Tina Shot Me Between the Eyes
and Other Stories

About the author

Jamaican-born Antoinette Tidjani Alou teaches French and Comparative Literature at the Université Abdou Moumouni de Niamey in Niger, where she has lived for more than two decades. She writes in English and in French, covering life-writing, poetry and short stories.

Tina Shot Me
Between the Eyes
and Other Stories

Antoinette Tidjani Alou

AMALION PUBLISHING

Published by Amalion Publishing 2017

Amalion Publishing
BP 5637 Dakar-Fann
Dakar CP 10700
Senegal
www.amalion.net

ISBN 978-2-35926-072-4 PB
ISBN 978-2-35926-073-1 Ebook

Cover image, a detail of *Iqra* (2016) by Omar Ba "Bao". Used by permission and courtesy of the artist.

Contents

Tina Shot Me Between the Eyes

Tina shot me between the eyes. I should have seen it coming, but I hadn't. In an epiphany of red, I discovered that I had gone too far. Then pain, too, went away as I gushed out, was catapulted up and away from my body. In a state of shock, I resisted the blue light. I could not leave. I hovered obstinately above the scene.

I linger still.

It is Tina who arrests me. I wish I could ask her why she did that. I wish I could tell her it's ok. That I don't mind, really, that I only want to understand. Although I am close enough to reach out and touch her, she too has moved beyond me. The scales have shifted. I am here and not here. I can no longer influence her or rough her up or gentle her or persuade her or do anything for or against her. She has become strong and alone and unfathomable.

She is frozen, now. Standing. Her hands are hanging by her side. The gun is still in her hand; a pretty, feminine, lethal little thing. Tina does not curl up in a corner, hunkered down on the fluffy bedroom mat like she used to when I would hit her and call her names – all the names in the book. All the names except the ones that were silent in my heart, or stuck at the back of my throat. All the names of Tina like a thick coating on my slow tongue. All of her names that would not slough off like a sordid confession: 'I love you Tina, baby, kitten, so take this and this!'

Tina is brown and thin all over except for her face, which is sharp and soft at once. Sharp in the centre, soft in the cheeks, strangely rounded on either side of that pixie nose, that pointed chin, those piercing dark eyes which ignite when she laughs or teases. For she used to laugh and tease. Sometimes. The light is gone out now and she is pale. But she is not crying. She is sitting on the bed.

I'm a mess on the floor. My blood and brains all over the place. I look like an exploded badly boiled egg, with no pretty gold yolk. My eyes are still there, wild. My small mouth is wide open in shock. I'm on my back, splayed. It's kind of funny.

I miss Tina already. I want to caress her cheeks. The cheeks I had learnt to slap. To enjoy slapping. But I find that I can't. It's the only thing that bothers me. That and how we got here in the first place. Why she lost it. Why she did it. How?

But she isn't looking at me. She is staring at the wreck in the bedroom. This is like a dream. Where anything goes. Not a bad dream, really. But, in truth, it is not a dream at all. I can see that. I will never again be able to wake up and touch Tina's face in anger or love. For I loved her, you know. I really did. But I, too, lost it.

It did not happen all at once. No. Once, life was almost perfect. Not quite, but that was because of Tina. It was as if her nature could not absorb perfection so she drew a line delineating how much happiness she could admit. I accepted her strangeness, having decided that it was part of her charm.

I am not sure how Tina and I got together in the first place. I do not understand it even now as my life, or rather hers, flashes in front of me. 'Flashes in front of me' isn't quite right, but I can't pursue that now. It's not a flash is all I can say. The shot between my eyes was a flash. This something I am experiencing is different. And I am right inside it, fading, but attracted still. Two black shiny magnets hold me here. They pull me in against themselves, irresistibly. I do not try to resist. I do not want to.

There is deep insight now. Speed, but no fury. No rush. A flash of visioning where time is no longer the thing that counts. Now, a time where other things happen otherwise; a weighing up that weight and density have gone. It's calm. It's all there. Tina and I, throughout the years, though years no longer count. Though...

~~~~~~~~

It was at the Young People's Retreat at Oberlin. Everybody in the Community called it the Singles' Retreat. This name was supposed to be a secret. It was a very infectious one, like so many other things in our Community, *their* Community, where it was almost impossible to keep anything to yourself. How Tina got to be a member in the first place is a mystery in itself. She is pious but also very private. Not overflowing and warm like most of the sisters and brothers. You can tell that from the way she hugs, the way she smiles. The opposite of Larry's bear hug or Sondra's melting embrace, her soft breasts against your chest for all of thirty seconds.

I had tallied it many a time. It was not only because I am a people watcher, not only because the Community was a lovely zoo. I say 'was', not because it has ended, but because after a while I couldn't take it and left, sick of all the holiness, all the togetherness. The Family Days. The Prayer Chains. The Young People's outings. It was at one of those that I first started to think about Sondra and to notice whom she was hugging and for how long.

She was warm and regular, Sondra-Miss-Thirty-Seconds, and sweet and innocent, too. She could afford to be, for she had never hugged herself. Did I eventually decide that she was not my type? Did God? Or was it Colin, now her husband, or Sondra herself, who had taken fate in hand? Who had sent me hunting for another potential mate in the small woods of the Community? Did I at some point decide that Tina was my type? Had she ever been my type?

Tina was nothing like Sondra. *Is* nothing like Sondra, not that I know what Sondra is like, really. I don't mean absolutely. I found out soon enough, from living with Tina, after we were married, that absolutely is for the other side where all is face-to-face, crystal clear and perfect beyond separation, conflict, anxiety, tears, longings. I simply mean that I didn't know Sondra that well, in her daily life. And, soon after Colin got into the picture, I started watching Tina instead.

The Community was large enough, over three hundred regular members, but few of us shared a roof and people went to different churches to leaven the dough of the world with the witness of their lives through the gifts of the Spirit. No one said it in these words precisely, but we all knew the mission and the expressions.

The Community was kind of endogamous, though, and dating opportunities were not many. Finding your sort was no easy thing either, except where religious fervour is concerned. The Community encouraged hotness since God abhors the lukewarm. He is passionate, an extremist who prefers the Saint or the Sinner. Fire or Ice; a firm choice: the fire of the Passion or the ice of refusal – passion in another guise, hard and dormant, gestating its heart of flame.

So, while there were many fiery females, a match was not easy. Married, engaged, too young, too old, already dating, not attractive, not interested, too new to the Community, not yet tested by Fire. But there was Tina. Tested. Proven. Single. Not dating. Right age. But strange. Was I interested and, maybe more importantly, could I interest her, become the man in the Community whom she would finally find arresting after all her years of membership?

It's not just Tina that was strange, the situation was too, for here I was contemplating courtship without the conviction that the lady was my type and without any idea of what profit, then, such a venture, if successful, would be. I had hit on her through a process of elimination rather than one of choice. I guess it was just the time of life, a longing for earthy roots even as I strove for heaven.

I played the guitar at Prayer Meetings; Tina was part of the Worship Team and sang on the choir. We sat not far from each other, but never together. Never. Not even after we were engaged then married. In fact, Tina and I never, ever sat together in church except on the day of our wedding. We were too busy serving on this or that committee. Always busy. Serving. Saving lives. Exchanging a few smiles.

It was at Oberlin that I first watched Tina laugh. Oberlin of the Vale, Oberlin of the Flame Trees, of the Orange Groves. Cool and sunny, buzzing and fragrant, serene and earthy. Oberlin. Our Retreat Place. Oberlin, where I first saw Tina laugh and laugh, pulsating under the flowering orange trees, with all of her body, all of her soul. Oberlin, where I first watched Tina grow from a thin quiet form, to the most substantially living vision that had ever blessed my sight.

I had no idea what had tickled her so, but there she was spouting laughter, moist and vibrant in the sunlight. I drew closer to her, suddenly possessed. I strained to join the circle around her. I wanted to enter it; the circle, her laughter. I wanted to enter Tina through the gateway of laughter. Immediately, I knew that I had to have her. In my life. In my apartment, barely furnished but paid for in full, with a large sunny balcony and sad spathiphyllia in mouldy terracotta pots. Did Tina of the crimson glee have a green thumb? Right there in Oberlin, I was ready to bet that she did, that she possessed every gift and grace and fruit of Spirit and Earth. My Tina. My Own. From that day and forever.

Forever, the time of the Community. No abstraction at all. The Kingdom had come, the Deliverer had come. Emmanuel was with us, God for us, forever, in us, with us, through us. Eternity was happening now and onwards, ever onwards, till the glorious meeting of every nation and tongue.

That day, too, would see birth and glory and trial.

Birth.

I wanted it. To bring forth, through Tina. A child of my loins, of her womb. I feared that word of flesh and blood and filth, but above all I desired it.

I was ready for courtship, for marriage, for family.

So, I wooed Tina.

It worked.

Our flash courtship was duly assessed and approved by my shepherd, David, by Tina's shepherdess, Betty, and by the Elders of the Inner Sanctum, headed by Vincent. Three months after Oberlin, when they announced our engagement to the assembled Community, I was there with my guitar in my hands, clutched as though I might lose it, and Tina was sitting on her chair among the choristers, occupying so little space. We did not stand together as prompted but merely bowed our heads to accept the benediction.

I was putting in long hours at my company at the time and could not help rubbing a tired spot between my eyes as I stifled a yawn. I had been up since 4 a.m. to begin the day with a leisurely Quiet Time and now, at 11 p.m., the Prayer Meeting was not quite over: the news of our engagement was the first of a long list of announcements that Vincent held in his long thin hands, shoulders stooped beneath his mop of white hair. Later, there would be carless sisters and brothers to drive home, then Tina to drop off. Then... Morning, again. Quiet Time. Maybe not so leisurely. Distracted, punctuated with wild yawning.

The Community took full charge of the planning of our marriage, leaving little for our respective families to do. The Community was our Family of God. We were in full agreement, Tina and I, but our families probably didn't see eye to eye with us in this. Mine did not matter so much, I was only the bridegroom, but for Tina's family, I am sure.

The marriage itself is hazy in my mind. If we can talk about a mind, in full view of my bits and pieces. They look ghastly and I can no longer clean. I used to be good, that way, around the house. But there is nothing I can do now about the mess I'm making.

Tina is hugging herself. The way she does when she is regrouping. The gun is now in the drawer of her bedside table. I watch her put it there, carefully. So, that is where she had kept it! When did she get it? How? Why?

Her head is down, but she is now standing. Her chin is tight, fighting back. Making a plan. I cannot touch her. I can. I am touching her, but she cannot feel it. I touch her chin, I try to make her look at me. "Tina, Tina..." I say, but she does not move, does not turn the bright magnets of her eyes towards me. They draw me in all the same, so I can see nothing else, nothing but her.

Her shoulders are covered. She is wearing her favourite tee-shirt. Almost the same colour as her skin. A brown woman in a brown tee-shirt. A wall flower. A criminal, now. And I am the victim.

Tina flashes before me as on the day of our wedding. A slender brown woman in a white dress that is frothy below the waist. A thin woman. Sparse. With bare shoulders and no hairstyle. Her hair is too short to do anything with, she says, and leaves it as it is. She wears no veil around her virginal face. Only a crown of pale pink rosebuds – a creation of one of the sisters, Heather, made with roses from her own carefully tended garden. Irrelevantly I remember winter thyme and sweet basil growing beneath Heather's kitchen window and Heather's veined hands making postcards and bookmarkers with fine dried floral elements. I do not expect Tina's delicate shoulders to be bare. I find the exposure disarming. She looks so small. Like a child. I cannot capture the fragrance of the rosebuds on her forehead, curled tight upon themselves like the tender fists of newborn babies clutching their secrets.

I want the ceremony to be over. I want to be alone with Tina. To take her away with me, at last, to sit her on my lap in the sparse comfort of the Ethel Room at Lethe, to nibble the soft skin below her earlobes, to lick the shell of her ears, to hear her sea song. I day-dream about Tina's crimson song. As the ceremony drags on and on, I remember her laughing in the sun at Oberlin.

We are going to Lethe for our honeymoon. Lethe. Tina and I and the grey mist on the green river, in another valley. Half of the Lethe Valley belongs to my family; though none of us live there now, the property brings in an honest income from ecotourism. We had lived there, my parents and I, for the first ten years of my life, tucked away in the heart of the island. I have travelled, some for studies then work, but after Oberlin, Lethe is my favourite place on earth. I will take Tina there so that she will come to know me. We will walk together in the misty valley where I grew up. I will teach her to make a body scrub with soft limestone. I will show her... But first the ceremony. The reception. The speeches.

My hands have always been a little wild. Exuberant, I spill red wine, inadvertently, on Tina's queenly attire. Down the centre of the white bodice a large, dark flower blooms. Tina is not happy. Her cheeks are as smooth as a baby's bottom, but she is not smil-ing. We will not have good photographs. The Family of God smiles encouragement, I smile back for both of us. Nothing can spoil this day for me, I think. I swell with pride, treasuring the way she had said, "I do".

But soon even I am no longer smiling. I had been happy, even after the mishap, happy that it would soon be over. That we could soon leave our three disparate families behind: representative members of Tina's family to the left; the Family of God, abundant, in the centre and, oh surprise, my entire family to the right, complete with uncles, aunts and cousins, all present, sitting a challenge to the Family of God, showing them.

There are too many people here. Too much music and song. Then dance. The opening dance. The many other dances. We dance, Tina and I. We dance and dance. With everyone.

I dance with Aunt Ethel. She is as tall as I am and no longer thin. We waltz, a close and distant couple, her belly separating and uniting us all at once. She tries to pull me over to the right wing where my family is massed. I slip through her grasp, escape into the dark, trying to get back to the centre. But my flight is not fast enough. The past arrests me. It slays me on my wedding day.

I stop for a moment to check my Timex watch. It has fluorescent hands. Tina's gift for my last birthday. It has an alarm that goes teet-teet-teet and prevents me from stressing about awaking too late for the Leisurely Quiet Time that is a must for all the Advanced Members of the Community. My watch agrees that the new couple may now slip away. I wink at it in the dark. I know that Tina must be tense, fearing the hour of reckoning, of the consummation of our marriage. My own tension is of another kind. I had had a life before the Community. A wild life that I had only hinted at once to the Assembly, out of necessity, before my Baptism in the Spirit. I was not proud of it, and my family had never been aware that there had been another me. Another Stephen.

I'm advancing to the centre to get Tina. To take her away with me to Lethe. I am still in the gloomy space between the right wing and the centre. I can see my family, thick as thieves, drinking, chatting with their heads together. I can hear them, I can tell their voices apart even with my eyes shut. They can no longer make me out in my dark suit in the dark. I hear a strong, low rumble. It's Uncle Dan, Aunt Ethel's husband. Aunt Ethel of the blue Ethel Room, the best room of the Eco Lodge at Lethe, a suite really, where I will take Tina.

Uncle Dan is peeved but reasonable. "After all, the boy is lucky," he says to a group of grumbling aunts.

My eyes are closed and I suppress a smile of sympathy for the boy he's defining with his moist meaty lips, with his farmer's hands. Strange hands for a doctor. I beam with a smile of affection for Uncle Dan. Good old Uncle Dan, God bless him. In the dark, I almost chuckle.

But Uncle Dan continues, in his voice that no one ever interrupts, "We are wrong to resent them, you know. Although, we got him young, he never did fit in with us, not like he does with *them*. They have *really* adopted him, with no whispering about weirdness behind his back. We should have told him all along, before it came to this. Blood is a strange thing. He must have felt it in his bones, all along".

I hadn't.

But I feel it now, like a chill. It leaves me hard and cool and naked.

I fetch Tina, wordlessly. I do not say goodbye to anyone. The assembled guests smile knowing, indulgent smiles at our retreating backs, so close together, suddenly. I drive to Lethe. I never tell Tina. I never thrash it out with my late family. I say nothing. What is there to say?

~~~~~

I do not try to talk to Tina now. I can talk, but no sound forms around my words. I cannot reach her. There is nothing I can do.

Perhaps Tina should do something to make this end. She does nothing. She does not scream or cry or faint or call the police or cover my body. Simply, she sits down once more on the bed; slowly, compulsively running her hands through her no longer short hair, sampling the texture, a strange absence on her face.

She had not been like that at Lethe, on the night of our honeymoon.

On our honeymoon at Lethe I had been as cold as ice inside, but I had wanted to make Tina feel. Had wanted her to laugh and laugh as she had done at Oberlin. I had wanted her to cry out to the night at Lethe; had wanted her to want me, to beg me to love her.

It worked.

For nine days and nine nights of Lethe, it worked marvellously. And I forgot for a while.

We returned to town, to my apartment, to work, to the Community, to life. To a life that gradually became impossible. But that was because of Tina, who was capable of only so much happiness, and because of the child, that would not come.

Tina has green thumbs. The large balcony of our apartment sprang to variegated life. She brought the spathiphyllia in, placed them in the soft light of the kitchen window. She changed the pots and the soil. She spoke about proper draining and not killing with kindness and smiled a knowing tender smile for their lustrous leaves. They rewarded her with indiscreet white flowers. Spathes, Tina corrected me gently, knowing.

After Lethe, I possessed Tina wildly, relentlessly, but she would not cry out. At Lethe, she had begged me. After two days of teasing, she had been desperate, no longer afraid; she had been crimson and flowing. I taught her many things and she taught me a few; things she never knew she knew. We had delighted in each other, watching the changing river from our window in the Ethel room.

Our marriage did not thrive in town. After Lethe, we were never again two, laughing together. In town, she never took me, never begged me. At the meetings of the Family of God, she would chant endlessly in tongues, tears rolling down her cheeks. I knew they were not tears of rapture. I knew that she was meeting frequently with her shepherdess, Betty, to pray that God would open her womb to give me the child that I craved. I knew that she too craved. I read her face as she watered her plants and beautified her apartment. Her apartment, not ours.

Small as she was she filled it almost entirely. It drove me crazy – the order, the beauty, the white walls, the bright carpets, the elegantly carved furniture from her family, her Indonesian rocking chair with delicately inlaid bronze flowers. It was too much, all of it; too much lustre and shine and colour. Too much housekeeping, and fragrance, and cooking. It was too full, all of it, except the empty room to which she brought nothing.

I stayed away as much as I could. She never reproached me for it. She never said anything. Not to me. Never. She had stopped working, fearing that the stress of her teaching job at St. Patrick's Primary School was getting in the way of our family plans. The classes were huge, the neighbourhood rough. She stayed at home, but nothing came of it. Well, nothing good.

I used to call her several times a day, as David, my shepherd had suggested. Of course, I had told him about the change in Tina, when she had stopped responding to me.

"Women are a mystery, Stephen," he had said to me. "They need words like the soul needs prayer. Like God needs adoration. You have to keep wooing her. Tell her you love her in the daytime, or she won't have you at night."

"God does not need anything, David!" I retorted sharply, contradicting, then suddenly ashamed. For David had mentored me throughout the years. He alone knew my story. And he had never judged or rebuked me.

David laughed. "He does, too!" He said. "God loves praises, just like a woman! Check your Bible!"

I did not check my Bible. I knew it by heart. I never went back to David. And I stopped calling Tina in the daytime.

But late one evening at the office, Lethe with Tina came back to me. The memory thrilled me like a good fix. I called home, but Tina was not there. I said nothing when I got in that night, earlier than usual, but I called every evening that week at the same time.

She was never there.

I started watching her. I called Betty, her shepherdess. Tina had not been meeting with Betty for counselling, although she went to community services regularly. With me. Each of us serving. Near. Apart.

It was at that time that the white walls of our apartment started filling up with paintings. Dark frames housing red, shapeless things. It was at that time, too, that Tina started bringing home a strange smell. Like turpentine and damp woods. She was seeing someone. He took her in his workshop. He smeared her with paint. She could not scrub it all off. Specks and smears remained. Small traces on her cheeks, under her fingernails.

On the day that I found out, I hit her. Hard. On the face, with the backs and palms of my hands. She cried out. It felt lovely – the sting on my hand, her cry, the percussion of flesh on flesh. I couldn't stop.

I stopped going to the Community meetings but continued to beat Tina fervently, like I used to pray. She never defended herself. She continued to come home to me, barren and besmirched. I chastised her. She cried out. I learnt new ways of hurting her, of hurting myself.

She got used to the pain, it seemed. Her body grew tight and silent. She would hunker down on the bedroom mat in a ball. Sometimes, I would have to pick up that frozen foetus and put it down on Tina's side of the bed. She would lie there like a huge pumice stone, while I murmured words of love, "O Tina, Tina, kitten, baby", into my pillow, on another sleepless night.

When our marriage entered the Valley of the Shadow, I stopped going to church as well. Tina went alone now, to Mass and to Community meetings, and she never told on me. At least no one ever called or tried to counsel me. I have no idea how she managed them, the Family of God. How she explained the bruises or the stains of paint. I continued to beat the hell out of her, but there was no pleasure in it now. No pleasure in anything.

Sometimes, Tina would remain frozen for an entire night. Then she would untangle herself and rise in the morning to care for her plants and her home. For me, too, because I was in it, in her home, and she never shirked her duties.

I understood her less and less. I feared her and I feared myself. I would die without Tina. Without her, our child would never come. I was breaking down at the office. Shooting up again, in the middle of the day. Beating the hell out of Tina, at night.

She would not leave her painter man. Her artist lover whom no one mentioned, whom I never mentioned, not once; not even when I was hitting her, not even the first time. She did not leave the Community or me. But she changed again.

She let her hair grow. A new look came into her black eyes; a look that defied me. She seemed to grow stronger, decided. Not content to let her suffer, her man was setting her against me now. But still, she stayed with me.

Well, she never left, but brought more and more paintings of formless red blobs into the apartment. They choked the life out of me. I chastised her. Routinely, now, not hot and angry anymore, but vaguely worried, with what was left of my mind. Vaguely. Confused.

Sleepless nights gave ways to listless days of weariness. I was yawning all day at the office. Today, the company doctor suggested I take a month off to pull myself together. Or even a sabbatical. I left the office at noon. I did not take my things. I was not going to take a month off. I was not going to go on a sabbatical. I was going to go home to Tina and beg her to forgive me, to help me. I could not trust myself to drive, so I called a taxi, gave my address and dozed off in the midday traffic.

The little snooze did me a world of good. As luck would have it, Tina was there. Her Mini Morris was parked in the first of our two spots on the parking lot. I would not have to hit her, I thought; we could talk today, like two normal people. Like man and wife.

I was wrong.

The reek of turpentine and damp woods met me at the door. Tina was standing with her back to the doorway. She was putting up a new painting. A painting on the Mercy Wall, the name I had secretly given to the only free wall in the apartment, right in front of the hallway. Why for Chrissake was she doing this?

I bellowed something insane, but she only turned and smiled at me and said, "Welcome home, Stephen. Do you like my new painting?"

It was the last straw! It was too cruel. Tina's mockery was demonic. To bring this here! This new painting was no red blob. The subject was quite clear. It was a portrait of my left heel, sticking out of a volcano; all that was left of me. I knew which foot it was because of the socks. I loved that pair of socks. The left foot had a hole in the heel, a big hole, but I could not bring myself to dump those socks and Tina refused to repair them ever again. All good and well; but this painting...

I would not be mocked in my own house; over my dead body!

I lunged for Tina, ready to revive the old techniques that would make her cry out. But she did not hunker down and wait for me to hurt her. In a flash she was in the bedroom. I stumbled after her, several paces too slow. She was already facing me, standing deadly still, the lethal little tool in her hands, pointed at my head.

Maybe I should have begged her then, but I couldn't believe it. I wanted to throw my head back and laugh and laugh, but dead serious, Tina fired.

I exploded in an epiphany of red.

Too late, too late, I beg her, "Christina, Christina ..."

But she cannot hear me.

And I cannot follow the blue light.

Odds and Ends

High noon last Friday, the 'But-will-it-arrive' garbage truck killed Booz Scato. From the back of the truck, an oddly conscientious sanitation worker shouted for the driver to stop. The worker, meaning to add the hot remains of the animal to the trash tumbling from the tipper, had just descended from his smelly perch when a crazy Old Lady, trampling on the hem of her flowered veil, abused him roundly in five languages – Hausa, Zarma, French, English and Jamaican creole – the last four of which he did not understand.

The Old Lady was stronger than she appeared. She shoved him aside and salvaged the body herself, scooping it up with the sheet of splintered plywood that the man had been using as shovel.

"But it wasn't my fault!" babbled the poor man. "Everybody saw the mutt run right into the truck. I wasn't going to leave it to rot in the street. But... anyway... the poor beast is dead, Mama!"

"Beast, y'rass!" the Old Lady shouted.

"I am not your fucking mother and this dog has a name!"

This outburst counted among her few words of grief, but for weeks on end those of her house could see the sombre work of sorrow. A dank silence limpened the people and the linen. The Old Lady's three domestic workers found the situation odd but not comical. They discovered that they could not banter about the events with the servants from neighbouring houses.

To see why, we have to start over – from the beginning.

The beginning. Now, that's a whopper. Where do you find the beginning of things? We create stories to fix our feet upon the earth that roils beneath us. We spin stories tirelessly; weaving an infinity of words that take us forward, take us back.

The beginning? A smelting together of odds and ends. If you are clever, a dreamer, or a trickster, you might make something magnificent out of the smidgens that we call life. Or you might try.

As for the dog, it was dead as lead, and there was nothing to do but to bury it.

～～～

Booz Scato's account – as told by Amina, the Old Lady's cook:

When I tried to help the Old Lady with the body, she insulted me for the first time in fourteen years of service, telling me go get my foolish r'ass out of the way. I wasn't used to cussing from the Old Lady. When saying so, she flew off the handle at the drop of a pin, but she didn't cuss, never dissed your father or mother when she got stink. She would light into you for what you had done, or not done, or done badly – which was usually the case, according to her. It would be reyrey about bad organization, slowness, and lack of initiative. She was harsh at times, but never foul-mouthed. You were always wrong, of course, but she never bore a grudge, and she paid well.

Bosscato – I could never say that senseless name like the Old Lady wanted – was three weeks old when he came to the house. He used to sleep on a soft worn-out wrapper of mine that I didn't have the heart to throw away. I was the first person he knew. That I was his mama is what the Old Lady's granddaughters, Amara and Akima, used to say when they came to spend the weekend.

When he was four months old, after his shots, I went home to bury my mother, leaving Bosscato in the hands of Soumaïla, the gardener. He looks big and crufty, Soumaïla, but he is a good sort. When I came back, Bosscato was all over me with his craziness. He just up and pissed on my leg like it was a tree trunk or a lamppost. Wallaï! I didn't get it, but I was happy to see him, too, so I didn't scold.

I am a Muslim, but I don't say my prayers, except at Ramadan, and when I was growing up in Benin, people didn't make a fuss about things like dogs and piss and all that. We had dogs and the kids pissed all over the place and people who prayed just picked out a clean place and life went on.

It's not like that over here. People hate dogs and treat piss like gunpowder. If a baby wets the floor, it's a big reyrey. Someone is sure to run for water to purify the spot. But serious, a baby's piss, – or a dog's shit – is like holy water compared to what some of them get up to on the sly. Humph!

The Old Lady had Amara and Akima's rumps bundled up in the big old diaper things they buy in the store, full of cotton that swelled up when the kids peed, and covered in plastic all over. She had them wear those things day and night, come heat, come harmattan. And the kids' mother was worse. The one Aisha, the housekeeper – heartless wretch – never gave the poor mites a break either, not even when the Old Lady wasn't looking. If it was her leg Bosscato pissed on, she would still be going on with a big reyrey up to today. Me, all I did was rinse my leg and give the dog a lick. He found it damned funny, too. Came back for more, yapping and laughing a dog laugh.

No, I really loved that dog. I liked looking after him because he was nice. He would eyeball you just like a person, with his head to the side. Really intelligent! He had a lot of things figured out.

When he was small, he discovered that he could pull low-hanging clothes right off the line. The Old Lady never let him into the house. He used them to make a crib for himself in the yard at night. The Aisha got fighting mad. She tried to hang the clothes up high when she had to leave them out, but he figured that if he jumped he could still get them. It became his sport at night when he was lonely. Some mornings the backyard was a mess of dirty rags. But the Old Lady never got rid of him, like that Aisha kept praying.

It hurt me bad to see Bosscato dead with his mouth open and his eyes like fish on ice. He was done for, but all of a sudden he was like a talisman for the Old Lady, too precious for me to touch, and she got stink on me in front of everybody.

That was damned out of order and unfair. I refused to talk to her for three days.

～～～

Soumaïla's version:

The Old Lady cussed Amina, dog-rotten, in front of the whole yard. She called me in a sweet girlish voice, like a river spirit, and I murmured the Ayat al-Kursi for protection.

"Ismaïl, my friend," she said. "We will have to bury him. Let's find a nice spot, at the back of the garden."

She acted as if we were going to plant a fruit tree. She never allowed me to plant anything special by myself.

The Old Lady gave strict instructions with a worried frown. When the hole – which she called the 'tomb' – was ready, she shooed me away with a slight wave of her hand like someone shedding a spider web.

She buried her dog alone, placed stones, branches and a wreath of bougainvillea on the mound of red dirt.

She went in without eating, without saying goodnight to her workers, without closing the house, and was never the same again.

～～～

Over the next forty days, the Old Lady went no further than her veranda, gave no instructions for the running of her house, did nothing, spoke little except to her children when they came to bring her a few necessities or when they came visiting – without their children who had been told that Grandma was resting. As this did not resemble their grandmother in the least, they thought to themselves that she was dead. But they could not imagine her silent and still.

The Old Lady's Story:

Sorrow spares no one; to be spared, you have to be good and dead. It is true that I loved that ugly old dog. I saw red when that stupid man tried to treat him like a piece of trash when he was still warm. Life is high and wide and you need a broad mind and a big heart to hold a tiny portion of it inside you. Only the thickest fools ignore this.

A dog is a living thing, just like people; when you get to know each other, you develop feelings, or even love. Species have nothing to do with it. No shepherd is surprised to learn that the Fulani herder loves his cattle. You may laugh at a gardener who talks to her plumbago, but once a gardener, you stop laughing. Naturally, you now console the scorched red ginger that must spend the day outside in the wicked month of May.

Really, I was low and it wasn't just about the dog. Trouble comes along like a pair of asses on the road, bearing a heavy load. More the ass you, you don't realize that they are coming to get you. The pair arrives and tumbles their load at your feet. Their bundles split open releasing memories that are not sweet, scattering needles that prick at old wounds. Ancient grievances sprout, and decrepit anxieties spring to vengeful new life.

For the first time since Amin's death, I don't feel the strength to weed and sow. But that is not why I keep to my room. As Amin would have said, I am on a retreat. Before Booz Scato died, I had started to slow down. Now all I want to do is sleep. Sometimes, I don't want to wake up at all. Sometimes, a feeble flame flickers. Definitely not the proverbial candle in the wind; I have lived a long life. I love the voice of Elton John, and his song about a candle in the wind used to move me although I don't care for the image itself. It makes me anxious. It's such an impossibly precarious position to be in. I think that when the time comes, you should just relax and go. But letting go is not in our genes; it must be cultivated. I am wavering like a woman who knows that divorce is a must, but who stops – for years – to clean the house. To leave things spick and span behind her.

~~~~~~~~

Epitaph by the Old Lady's daughter, Hyrama, Amara and Akima's mother:

Last night at eight I found Mama dead in her bed. I don't know how or why she did it. She used to tease us with her deathbed scenarios, with the family gathered around, and she, the star as always, consoling us in advance, half-tender, half-mocking, lessening the pain of her impending departure. She would bow one last time and leave with a satisfied smile on her lips. Knowing Mama, I had no trouble buying that story.

But it wasn't like that at all. Mama died all alone and there was no smile on her face. Her room was clean and fresh, her books and papers tidy on the nightstand. The top sheet was stretched firm and tight up to her chin. A hint of Flower by Kenzo floated in the air. The fuzz of Mama's grey hair was gathered primly in the fine mesh of a hairnet. But a frown of deep perplexity creased her brow.

I had missed the end of my mother's story and feared that there was unfinished business despite the cold evidence of her silent form.

Eighteenth Sunday in Ordinary Time

I t was no ordinary Sunday. In fact, it was Saturday evening, and soon it would be time for anticipated Sunday Mass. As canon law allowed it to be Sunday after 6 p.m. on Saturday, Mina and other parishioners of Our Lady of Perpetual Help in Niamey could go to Sunday Mass on Saturday evening, sleep in on Sunday morning, and devote the rest of Sunday to non-ecclesial pursuits. With three young daughters who blessed her heart but drained her energy, Mina found anticipated Sunday Mass very convenient.

It was August; the height of the rainy season, a time when the Sahelian climate and the Catholic liturgical calendar were at variance. On this eighteenth Sunday in ordinary time, all day thick white rain had scourged the thin soil of the Sahel, engorging River Niger, destroying earthen dwellings in town and country.

The Da Silvas, Mina's neighbours who hailed from Togo, were not going to Mass today, but Mina knew that she would go, unless there was a flood. The rain had calmed the children and the entire household had yielded to sensuous slumber for most of the afternoon.

"An umbrella and a sweater were all it would take to get there," Mina thought. Ali, her husband was abroad, but any member of his family who dropped in with a car would drive Mina to the cathedral, or she would take a route taxi.

Toward the end of the afternoon, the downpour diminished, but the bodies of the people, of the trees, and the animals still remembered the hours of fury. The people shivered, the trees quaked and hummed in the last throes of prolonged climax, and the animals moaned softly or were silent – even the birds, who thought they owned the garden and cared little for anyone's rest were subdued into muteness.

The parishioners of Our Lady of Perpetual Help Cathedral were cold. The proper name, Our Lady of Perpetual Help, honouring Mary the mother of Christ and making her the patron of a people perpetually in want of divine succour, was hardly ever used by anyone: the parishioners simply called their parish church 'the cathedral' and the majority Muslim population of Niamey dubbed it 'Kaba Kwara', the house of the Bearded Man, an affectionate tribute in Songhay-Zarma language of the West to Monseigneur Berlier, the founding father of the parish and the subsequent archbishop of Niger's small Catholic community. The parishioners, shunning proper appellation, hugged themselves, gratefully remembering that God dwells everywhere: in mosque, in church, and in their own abodes, however humble. Today, three of every four parishioners who habitually opted for anticipated Sunday worship on Saturday evening praised this effect of divine omnipresence. Glorifying God for the bounty of cool damp air in a hot dry land, they decided to keep their feet clear of the *poto-poto* of Niamey; they would not go to Sunday Mass this week. God was good. The day was rich. Free air-conditioning flowed from heaven for one and all, inside and outside. Here, finally, was equality; if only it would last.

"Adam must be happy today," Mina thought, imagining her neighbour Hawa's fat-cheeked boy who nearly died when he was three from drinking the kerosene oil in a Fanta bottle that Hadiza, Mina's household help had left lying on the ground in the backyard. Hadiza would never listen; she knew it all. Adam had enjoyed the three May days spent at the Gamkalley Clinic with Hawa hovering by his bed, forking out more money than the family could afford to save her first son. Adam had loved the clinic because of the attention, the numerous visits of family, friends, and neighbours, but chiefly because of what he called the 'good thing'; the thing that neither Mina nor Hawa could afford: the cool air that hummed by night and day from an old air-conditioning unit, soothing the child's feverish body, vanquishing the scorching of the month of May.

When Adam was out of danger and home again, in the furnace of May, the two women, Mina and Hawa, had laughed, fanning themselves in the warm shadow of a mango tree, with a sigh in their voices over Adam's unfortunate love of good things – and their own.

"Adam must be sleeping now," Mina thought with a smile for the plump rambunctious boy as she made her way to church, the spear of her furled umbrella prodding the compacted sand of her yard, her cautious steps picking across the last wet stretch of evening.

∼∼∼

The cathedral, infinitely less lofty than its name implied, was a sparsely planted field beyond the perimeter of the altar, whose sacred precincts registered full professional presence – entirely male and primarily priestly. They were all there, as if in compensation for the abdication of the laity: the black and the white, the lean and the hefty, the shiny and matte; the priests and a deacon of God, flanked by two teenaged altar servants. Today their varied complexions and forms were, in the main, as matte as the expensively painted living room walls of well-to-do Kwara Kano housewives. Even Father Augustine, who habitually shone from oblong head to yam-like neck, appeared cool and powdered. The pores of the faithful and those of their shepherds enjoyed a short seasonal respite – the fat below the skin, for those who had any, sat like margarine in a fridge; it did not melt and ooze. Today's daytime temperature averaged twenty degrees Celsius. A cold wet day in the Nigerien Sahel.

Mina is not complaining. She blesses the weather. Everyone in the Sahel loves rain, but Mina, moreover, relishes matte; her aesthetics are not those of the continental traditonists, she takes no pleasure in the sight of shiny skin. She finds Father Augustine infinitely more personable when he is not mopping his baldpate and fighting a losing battle with diction and shine. Today, Father Augustine is saved by grace, or Mina is. Above the collar of his priestly robe the ebony skin of his thick neck, long head, and ovine face are as dull as Mina's old Tuareg bracelet. And he is not saying the homily.

~

Eighteenth Sunday in Ordinary Time, Year A, approaching the end of a long wild day at the peak of the brief rainy season. August. Niger's month of bounty, Inch Allah. At noon darkness shrouded two thirds of the land. Light fled, ruddy and ominous to the east, chasing the wind before it, playing foul, giving no warning to the trees.

"Transfiguration," Mina thought. In her fourth rainy season in the Sahel, she still found the swift shift from morning, or noon, to fiery twilight magical. For as long as she could remember, Mina had loved to watch the rain come down, provided there was no stab of lightning or blast of thunder. The lightning, she feared, could make her go blind, completely, and even her father, her childhood hero, did not like the thunder.

No living creature does. In West Africa it is the roar of the deity whose name no one takes in vain, which few pronounce. Dongo. Shango.

"Dance," Mina thought, chilly and spellbound, watching the mounting wind toy with the trees. Anticipating. But the trees did not seem merry. Possessed, they soon rocked and howled, or cracked and broke. When the Ponciana, the Terminalia, and the Neem trees of her garden thrashed in wild salute, bowing and groaning, flexing and snapping, firing missiles, ejecting birds and nests like tainted fruit, Mina's mind turned to the Last Day.

"Wind and rain," Mariama, Ali's sister said, peering out into the darkness, beyond the iron slats of the shutters that guarded the glass panes of the front door, "Poor people are going to get a beating today. Mud houses are going to fall." But Mina's mind could go no further than her own house, which was holding up, and her garden, flayed and savaged by the elements.

Dusty wind stung the eyes of the thick-lashed camels after a two-day lull in the rainfall, but now the rain was back. It swooped down on the wings of the wind, landed, and slapped the earth mightily like a vengeful parent quieting hungry children.

It was serious rain, like those of Mina's childhood. It made her hungry for the comfort foods of her distant homeland, of her small tribe: boiled green bananas, which are nothing like the sweet ripe fruit. These must number several dozens to feed a family of seven or eight; two or three generous hands of almost mature, unripe banan-as, slender and full, separated one from the other by her mother's swift delicate fingers, leaking stain onto the blade of the knife, the kitchen bitch, scored down one seam and plunged into an alumin-ium basin of water to await peeling and boiling and melting on the palate, if they had been chosen and cooked by a discerning – a de-manding – mother, blending with the seasoning of salted mackerel, fried up with scotch bonnet peppers, scallion, garlic, thyme, cherry tomatoes – ripe and juicy, red and flavourful – fresh black pepper, ground in a small wooden mortar with an iron pestle, country coco-nut oil, borderline, not yet rancid, not quite new; perfect.

"That's the beauty of the thing," Mina's mother would say, vaunt-ing the strange human taste – or was it only that of the poor among them? – for a touch of the carrion.

The family would huddle together and chew in meditative si-lence as white rain thrashed the house, battered the roof, rattled the windowpanes, drummed into bodies, and leaked with loud plops into the pails and basins set out to catch the deluge. Serious rain meant that the heavy plodding, sliding, and falling of children, that the pleasure of the slick and suck of the new mud, would have to wait till later, when the rain subsided to a drizzle.

~~~~

Eighteenth Sunday in Ordinary Time, Year A, Mina arrives late for Mass. The taxi drivers, too, are staying home, evading the slushy streets. At home, they imbibe the erotic aroma of incense-wielding wives, ostensibly to warm the house and cleanse septic odours; surreptitiously, they sniff the burnt perfume that seeps itself into nooks and crannies, into places seen and unseen. Feigning indifference, their hands, in secret, travel to the middle of their djellabas, as they think of places unseen, relishing the eloquent entreaty of meat spiced with the aphrodisiac *dakan maza*.

The church, a sparsely planted field, swells to more generous dimensions around the altar. Swinging incense in a bronze censor, Father Ambroise, the chief celebrant, circles the holy space. His circle completed, he faces the aisle and incenses the people. Mechanically, he swings the censor, once, twice, thrice, and bows, like a housewife sweeping for the tenth time in the day, her mind on other things. He does not think that, symbolically, he is making the congregation an offering, holy and acceptable unto God, or that he is inviting them to offer themselves as such. The diminished ranks of the faithful bow in response with stiff nervous necks, shivering their sacrifice, some checking their watches, all wishing that the priests would get on with it and release them to the warmth of their beds.

Mina buttons her pink sweater all the way up. Her ankles, like her throat, is a weak point in her body, and the sweater sits low, scooped to her collarbones. Her wax print ankle length skirt-suit was not a good choice; its puffy baroque sleeves were not studied for enclosure in the narrow confines of a sweater.

The entrance hymn has been sung, the penitential rites are over, the Gloria has ended in a shame-faced slide under the damp pews as Mina slips inside the humble headquarters of the archdiocese of Niamey, and Isaiah the Prophet promises free water to the thirsty; not just water, but wine and milk as well; at no cost. Mischievous, Mina's mind declines the offer of milk; after four years of reserving it for the girls, she no longer digests it.

~~~

"Why spend your money for that which does not satisfy?" The hoarse voice of Angelina questions gruffly, in empathy with the God of the prophet. Defiant and strong at the lectern, Angelina stands her ground, her broad back turned to Father Ambroise. An anachronistic Paulian who abhors the presence of females beyond the front pews of the church, Father Ambroise is also a passionate opponent of girls serving on the altar and of women reading the scriptures during Mass. He suffers the new mother who plays Mary in the Christmas pageant – it's only once a year – but swells up like an angry bullfrog at the sight of half-dressed girls performing the so-called Eucharist dances, endangering the sacred offerings they shimmy down the aisle, distracting the men, and making a pop-py-show of the Christian cult in the eyes of the majority Muslim population.

But today not a soul is dancing. No girls in short wraparounds with knees and navels showing will wiggle impertinent buttocks down the sacred aisle, their black teenaged faces striped and dotted with white kaolin, grinning idiotically. Today, there is no rocking in the pews to Ho Lung's Gloria, which has travelled all the way from the Caribbean to Africa, to Niamey, Niger; where no one knows that Father Ho Lung is a Chinese Jamaican of Buddhist ancestry, or cares that such oddities exist. There is no provocation save Angelina's husky voice, so today Father Ambroise's fat spirit might have settled relatively unprovoked among the folds of his priestly attire were it not for the beastly girthing of his cincture. Invisible beneath the inner tunic of his alb, and the outer garb of his chasuble, the symbolic tether of the cincture, belting him to the will of God, was biting into his belly bottom with an annoying hardness.

Mina looks vaguely at the circle of priests that fans out in a semicircle of chairs behind the altar, below the cross, bereft of the striking effigy of the crucified Christ. Why? Is this so that the Muslims will not take Catholics for idolaters? Mina wiggles her toes to stay awake. As she listens Angelina's harsh voice moistens with the words of the Prophet Isaiah, in chapter 55. "Eat that which is good, relish fat meats, and be full!"

"Oh, yes Lord! Amen!" The laity stir and murmur, chasing pins and needles from their feet and buttocks, "Solid food today!" their hearts enthuse.

Angelina's mouth waters for the succulent enticements of God. A promise is a promise, and she takes promises seriously. But as she reads, it occurs to her that this is really a bargain: "Hear and your soul shall live: and I will make an everlasting covenant with you…" The Almighty is offering free and delicious sustenance in return for an "everlasting covenant". You couldn't just eat the food and run, throwing over your shoulder the Hausa proverb claiming that those who stay when the food is done are nothing but gossips. You couldn't wipe your mouth and leave, closing your ears to the collective proverbial taunt that those who run when food is done have no shame. No, eating this Word was like swallowing a rope and an anchor; it was binding. Be mine, forever.

Angelina squints warily at the Word, contemplating the wiles of God. Angelina's feet trip against the stone of the Covenant. There is a protracted pause in her reading, but the faithful, concentrating on keeping warm, do not notice. Looking beyond Angelina, beyond the fat flickering candles flanking the altar, Mina pats the bundle of her baroque sleeves inside her sweater. Her mind wanders to Ali, the children, and the wreck of her garden.

Angelina is caught in the web of the words she is delivering. She knows that she is unfit for enduring bonds and so has not married, preferring a pet to a husband; a tomcat, always. She knows that such a relationship is only for a time, that the tomcat's nature will ultimately carry him howling off into the night, beyond the confines of her neighbourhood in Mawrey, so far that he will not find his way back to her house, to the foot of her king-size bed, when his lust abates. Knowing this, Angelina has never named a pet, not even to call him "Tom" or "cat". She simply says, "you there", to each successive feline companion; regardless of its coat, habits, size, or shape, it's always "you there"; in love, or chiding, or invitation to supper.

A devoted lector, all week Angelina meditates the text she will read at Sunday Mass. She does not relish this week's reading. Covenants are not her thing. She does not think that she will ever grow into a liking for them.

"The flesh is weak," she nods in her heart. "Look at David, the passionate singer of the psalms, the Jewish Sufi, the handsome redhead, the servant of God; even he did not pass the test!"

Slices of the life of David, her favourite among the Patriarchs, flash in an instant through Angelina's mind. Sensuous, King David had spied on Bathsheba in her bath of monthly purification, and had not averted his eyes before the vision of wasted ripe splendour – her foolish husband was fighting at the front in the king's own army. David the Mystic, God's confident chick, a bard forever and ever, had stared lustingly at another man's wife; he had plotted and stolen her, deliberately sending her husband, a captain in his army, to his death. David's singing and dancing, his hymns of praise, his compositions for the harp and the cithara, the opening of the plump rosebud of his mouth unto the Lord like a nestling waiting for a worm from its mother, had not spared him from the fangs of the flesh.

Angelina is forewarned of the guiles of God and of the weaknesses of the body. Half Nigerien only, by blood, being born of a Togolese mother, she is fully Nigerien by law and taste: she loves her meat, and is Muslim in her habits of personal hygiene. Angelina is torn. She wants to feed her soul on fatness, but the bait is in the meat. People are so complicated and God is so demanding; who can make the grade?

Mina flexes her neck to relieve tension. It cracks. The alleluia sung, with no real conviction in the absence of the better part of the choir, Deacon Bonaventure proceeds to proclaim the gospel. He does so in a reedy fluting, rocking forwards and backwards on his spindly legs, relishing his moment of glory.

After water, milk, and meat, God is now laying on fish. The lone Frenchman in the church inwardly condemns this order of service, the putting of fish after meat in a meal is not done, but the Beninois and Togolese are paying rapt, empathetic attention. Fish, the food of kings; fish, the bounty of the sea – eternal queen, beneficent mother – fish galore! Faithful, they have braved the rain to hear the Word, can you imagine, hunger biting their guts, but their hearts abiding in the right place. For it is just and right to give Him praise, but they have eaten no solid meal since morning, nevertheless, here they are, shuffling on foot, following Him, singing hosannas till their voices break. And there He is, not proud at all, knowing everything. And He gives them bread to eat. And fish!

They eat till they can eat no more, and there are twelve baskets of remains. Twelve! Did the guests of that historic fish feed, that most relevant of miracles, take back some of the leftovers for those at home, for the dogs, for the pigs, for the morrow? No, maybe not for the animals. But you have to think ahead and save, save, save.

Mina knows that doggy bags are not allowed when it comes to food from heaven.

"Holy meals are perishable; manna is for the day at hand, nothing for tomorrow, for it is promised to no man!"

Mina smiles to herself. Pity, she is not a priest; she would have been a better preacher than Father Ambroise and Father Augustine put together. And she loves fish. Or thinks she does, for she has no idea of the heights of passion that fish can inspire; she is not Togolese or Beninoise, she was not raised by mothers of these nationalities.

The parishioners who answer to that description are now fully and resolutely awake.

"Fish, plenty fish! Fish from the sea of heaven! The Bible says that in the beginning the sea and the sky were one. One and the same; until God separated the waters that were above the heavens from the waters that were below the heavens; and called the one sea, and the other sky. And now all the waters have reunited, and fish rain down upon the land. God is bountiful; nothing like those tight-fisted priests, sitting in high places. The fatter, the meaner; gaping mouths full of 'God will provide!' loving their food and their beer".

Deacon Bonaventure is party to this wholesale judgement of the priests near whom he sits, facing the scanty pews. His head bowed in self-imposed penance, he traces a small cross over his slack belly.

"No matter how bad they may be, we mustn't condemn the priests."

He frowns then lifts his white head to the pulpit where Father Ambroise is clearing his voice in preparation for the homily. Across the street, near the market that the congregation can smell when the wind turns, wafting in the odours of rotting cabbage and the pestilence of damaged smoked fish, the cackle of a loudspeaker warns that the muezzin of the Zongo Mosque is about to call other more numerous faithful to Maghrib prayers.

Mina imagines Baba Koda's bony shins wet with water from his ablutions and smiles. Baba Koda is Ali's uncle. The Zongo Mosque, where he will say his prayers, was established by his father, Ali's grandfather, when he came down from Sokoto, to win souls for Allah. Mina imagines Baba Koda, taking one last draw on his Craven A cigarette, before crushing the butt and entering the mosque. She smiles again, a mocking daughterly smile, and returns to her own worship.

~~~~~

Fishing his fat paws out from his sleeves, Father Ambroise begins to preach. The provisional unity of the gospel acclamation dissipates. The parishioners resort to the lethargic expediencies of sleep or daydreaming – the invariable fruits of Father Ambroise's monotonous homilies. While they rest in the Spirit, the hefty cleric drones interminably, holding forth like a bumblebee, with total disdain for the notion of 'short and sweet'.

The faithful of Our Lady of Perpetual Help have no luck with priests whose names begin with 'A', for the wiry Father Albert is another phenomenon. He does not despise female service in the church beyond the front pews as fat Father Ambroise does; his problem is with the poor. They gather at the doors of the Catholic Mission like flies and never bestir themselves in gainful labour. His brother cleric, Antoine, the third plague of our Lady of Perpetual Help, gives everything away, everything short of the holy vessels and clerical robes, but only to Muslims; never to Christians. The two men never agree, except when it comes to Father Ambroise's homily: the brother does not have the gift of predication; something should be done to restrain him.

Clara, however, has the antidote for Father Ambroise's soporific drone. Clara is alert, though distant. She is keeping watch with her Lord. Her head is cocked at the angle of sanctity. Her huge heavy-lidded brown eyes, lifted to the sky, are momentarily arrested in their celestial flight by the sooty ceiling. Persevering, though, they breach the barrier of steel and concrete, and widen in contemplation of the Lamb. Clara is oblivious of the envious and the hard-hearted. He has melted her heart of stone, giving her a heart for love alone. She hears the call. She is ready to be sent; to be persecuted, to be burnt at the stake, to fall asleep tonight and never wake up.

Clara's upturned eyes see the Glory. She beholds, in the company of John the Divine, great crowds returning from the long tribulation. They have washed their soiled garments in the blood of the Lamb, and now shine with a heavenly glow. Alleluias burst into blossom. Incense goes up. People of every nation, land, and creed worship the Lamb of God, as Catholics call Jesus.

An Apocalyptic angel holding a seal reads off, in the purest Hausa accent of Kano, the endless list of redeemed Sahelians of all creeds. A long shudder convulses Clara's solid frame while the multitudes chant and cheer, forgetting manmade distinctions. A bouquet of song bursts from Clara's heart, it floods her arteries, suffuses her with fire from head to toe. Clara, blood red, flits down a pathway of clouds. Her heart burns within her. She does not feel the strain of her cervical muscles; she does not hear the protest of her neck bones. She is blind to Mina's mocking gaze. Never more will she crave the bodies of men. No, never more; never more. Her boss may have to fire her, but it's over. She will not exchange her favours to keep her job. She will not submit to another woman's husband – and not a fetching one at that. With Michel, it's over, too; never more will he poke her with his skinny dick and pointed hipbones, then sated and selfish, roll over and sleep off the Saturday afternoon, with his wide mouth open, drooling.

Clara's heart batters against her ribs, batters the cartilage of her temple until lightening flashes from within and she crumples softly to the cold tile floor of the humble cathedral, so softly that Father Ambroise does not hear her, and presses on, with a new keenness in his voice.

Clara's head misses the wooden pew where she is now resting, the pleats of her prim white skirt folded around her sturdy shins. A rustle of whispered comments, a brief issue of malice froths and subsides, and Mass continues. The shadows of the Neem trees brush the lean sides of the church; people yawn, stretch, scratch themselves, blink, and open their eyes in preparation for communion. If only Father Ambroise would wrap up the homily.

Father Ambroise's name alludes to the favourite food of heathen gods. He loves wine, but, for a Beninois, is strangely indifferent to fish. The miracle of Cana is understandably a great favourite of his, but fifteen minutes into the homily, the Spirit warms his heart. Here is an offer of free food for the Sahel. New compassion swells beneath his robes and he almost chuckles.

"Antoine must be in his element today," he smiles in his heart, with rare affection for this fellow priest, a great lover of fish.

Father Ambroise's new vibrancy fails to cheer the chilly congregation. His voice flows out the doors (there are no windows), or catches in the dark corners of the semi-vacant church.

"Brother and sisters, where is our faith? With next to nothing, Jesus feeds five thousand men, not to mention the women and children!" His robed arms flail the air, floundering for inspiration.

Mina, sorely provoked, resists the mounting scorn she feels for Father Ambroise. She gives a grade of 0/20 in exegesis to this eater of meat and drinker of wine.

"Tell us how many people Jesus fed, you f…" Mina checks her profane anger. Her right fist is tight; clutching the imaginary whip she longs to take to the fat cleric's back.

"What would religion come to without the women and their children?" Mina fumes.

"For every man in the Church, how many women and children are there? Come on, man, give us an estimate of the mighty crowd that Jesus satisfied! Are you blind or just plain dumb?"

The fear of God's displeasure holds Mina's judgemental flight in check. Mentally, she waylays the priest to give him a piece of her mind after the service. But she is tired of airing her opinions to the clergy. So she changes tactics and composes in her mind a stirring homily on women and children in the Church, extolling the silent majority and the example of Jesus in their regard; so different from that of the Church, which would collapse without the females of the fold.

Dead silence grips the congregation. The women and children are resting in the Spirit. Whether the homily includes or excludes them, they are there – along with a few men who seem to find nothing amiss with the bias in the celebrant's preaching, or in the biblical inventory.

"Where is our faith?" Father Ambroise questions.

"Why the wars and rumours of wars? The genocides. The hunger. Why?"

"Well, Father, 'give them, yourself, food to eat!' " Mina sulks.

"Even so, man shall not live by bread alone," Father Ambroise backpedals.

"True word; fish is far better," murmurs Jean-Baptiste, a skinny spare parts dealer, to the kneeler before his back pew.

"But fried locusts are good, too; crunchy, with lots of pepper," he adds mentally, for he was born and raised in Niger and knows no other homeland.

Jean-Baptiste smiles as he thinks of what he would like to eat for supper tonight: tiny sprat fried crisp, laced with red palm oil, fresh hot peppers crushed, and newly steamed *ablo* maize cakes, light and fluffy, with just a hint of sweetness. His mind still on food, he wonders how the fish in the gospel was cooked, the fish that Jesus used to feed the multitude. His fervent hope is that it was not roasted; he hates the taste of roasted fish. But with all this rain, there will be no *ablo* tonight; the firewood needed to steam *ablo* for hours will be soaking wet, or damp and smoky.

"No *ablo*," Jean-Baptiste sighs as Father Ambroise's arms swoop down, searching for the concluding statements of his homily.

Then, he remembers! No, he cannot conclude; not yet. The congregation will have to wait some more for communion. Father Ambroise has one final exhortation. A serious one. The large cleric takes a deep breath and plunges head first.

"You must forsake idolatry!" he buzzes, then searches for a connection to the day's readings.

"It is because of your talismans and charms, because of your witchcraft and wickedness, that you hunger and are not fed; that you suffer and are not healed!"

There, he has said it.

He peers into the thin gathering, but can discern no effect on the closed faces of this headstrong flock.

"God is the healer, and not the marabout; we are saved by the blood of the Lamb and not by that of sacrificial rams!"

Father Ambroise falters, doubting for once, his choice of words. Will that pack of goats believe that lamb or ram it is all the same?

"In the name of the Father and of the Son and of the Holy Spirit..." he concludes with sullen rage in his heart.

After all, the battle is not his, but the Lord's; God help him!

"There we go again!" Mina groans under her breath. "Lord forgive me, but the man is a fool! Why can't he leave the damn healers alone, seeing that he himself can provide no food for the people, no inspiration of any kind, human or divine?"

Father Ambroise is finished. The congregation utters a grim "Amen." The people are polite, but obdurate. The Mass draws into the last quarter. A glint of obstinacy sparks in the eyes of the wearers of portable protection. You never know on which bank of life your luck will surface. Africa has its mysteries. Give unto God that which is God's....

The wearers of amulets, charms, and other portable protections clench their teeth. They clasp their secret armaments: against misfortune, against evil tongues and evil eyes, against contrary winds, sterility, spirits of heat and cold; against the sicknesses of the body and of those spirit, against the words of the fat priest whose family back home in Benin are adepts of the Godess of the Sea.

They clutch their gri-gris tight. They take their portable protection everywhere.

Soon, they will walk them up the aisle to Holy Communion.

Eating and Drinking and Raising Hell

For Bill Gillen and Connie Gillen

❝I hope that the dinner that Awa will make to announce your engagement won't be a remake of her mother's fiasco," my mother, Nana said. Her face is drawn tight. Yet my siblings and I smiled conspiratorially at the allusion to a well-known community yarn.

I knew that Nana has misgivings about more than the dinner party. I was getting engaged to Awa, the daughter of Miss Mary who did not fit in, and who seemed impervious to collective disapproval. For Nana, marriage is above all a family affair: a matter of bloodlines, breeding, and discernment. She was not satisfied with Awa's credentials. I was intent on marrying Awa, I wanted this union more than I had ever wanted anything in life, but I saw no need to be brutal with my mother.

"Oh, Nana," I said, a steadfast smile screwed to my face, coaxing her indulgence, "men no longer marry simply to keep a cook at hand. Luckily, I've had enough good home-cooking to last me a lifetime. For we all know about the culinary tradition at Miss Mary's. But Awa herself ...."

My mother's face furrowed into a frown that did not encourage developments on the qualities of my beloved, so I decided to take a rain check. Nevertheless, as I trudged through the damp vegetation in the direction of Old Man Theo's land, my mother's words kept echoing through my mind, advising against much more than a remake not only of the unconventional dinner that Awa's mother, Miss Mary, had given two and half decades ago to announce to Howard's Grove her engagement with Big Enoch; Big Enoch whom she never should have countenanced in the first place, not that she could be picky. No, it was more than the dinner. No one ever voiced it, but the village, despite grudging respect for Miss Mary's spunk, has never really accepted what it sees as her unusual lifestyle.

Miss Mary, a woman from proper Howard's Grove, had not only given a most unfitting dinner party, she had, moreover, misbehaved dreadfully on the subsequent Promise Walk, the nocturnal promenade that the village allowed the new fiancés, for no more than one digestive hour. Miss Mary had disrespected the tradition; she had erred and had not repented. So, it wasn't so much about Awa herself; nor was it about me. It was about Miss Mary, and about me marrying Miss Mary's daughter.

What was it that set Miss Mary apart, making her one of us yet different, familiar but not at all *ordinary*?

Ordinary is a very positive word in Howard's Grove. It is the way to be: plain speaking, straightforward, and modest, with nothing to hide from God or man. And here I was, a man from Howard's Grove, hopelessly in love and about to be publicly engaged to a girl whose mother was exceptional. And we all know that things like that run in the family. Both mother and daughter were given to hearty demonstrations of mirth. Awa's mother was no cook, and neither was she. Worse, neither was afflicted by this state of affairs that elicited Nana's most scornful grunts. Somehow, it seemed, marrying Awa was like marrying Miss Mary and living her story all over again.

I had heard the story of Miss Mary's dinner party many times, although it had happened over twenty-seven years ago in sleepy Howard's Grove, two years after I was born, when Awa was not yet a twinkle in her father's eye. It was as if I had attended Miss Mary's dinner party, had sat, a grown man, at her strange table, and had enjoyed her remarkable food. The day after, I had not understood the rumpus about Miss Mary and Big Enoch breaking the rules of the Promise Walk.

Howard's Grove does not share my views. I believe that the old people must still mutter:

"How could Mary have dared to desecrate the Promise Walk and remain so natural, and seem so pure? And what made us condone it?"

Silent resentment is a way of Howard's Grove, or mute questioning, or voiceless awe. Never forgetting is another of its traits while compiling black lists is its favourite sport; that and disregarding the rest of the world. No doubt my name and Awa's will soon be lettered in to the community's bad books.

Nana's disapproving presence was heavy with guilt, tongue-tied with discretion. It was she who had chosen to name me Enoch. But biblical names were common, back in the day, even before the straight-laced era in Howard's Grove. I was her first son and she had wanted for me a name of strength and goodness, somehow forgetting – in the glory of motherhood, in the power of naming, in the shadow of Spirit – the other Enoch, the one who had long since disappeared; the stranger, the farm hand, who had married Miss Mary, or whom Miss Mary had married – a handyman, her aunt's servant.

<center>~~~~~</center>

Of the past I knew the oft-repeated narratives, but for the future who can tell? Awa's mother's story, the story of the mother of my beloved, the story of Miss Mary, had a presence that would not subside. Latter-day Howard's Grove wouldn't let it. I myself was not particularly worried about it, but the Grove more than compensated for what they construed to be my lack of good sense by raising the past before my every step. These last weeks, the Grove has forced me to revisit the day that supposedly holds the portent of what my life with Awa will be. But the gloomy Grove cannot erase the smile that teases my lips, that creases my eyes, at every thought of Awa.

I cannot say which version of Miss Mary's story is the true one, nor what is true and what is false in all that has been said about the night self-righteous Howard's Grove found itself eating and drinking and raising hell, as Old Man Theo had repeated many times in my presence when I was still a child, his whole leg stretched out in front of him, his half-a-leg resting on a tree stump polished by time and sorrow.

I had always associated Old Man Theo with that tree stump. It seems that there was an agreement between the man and the felled tree; that the two were going to the grave together. The old man had been stubborn about felling the tree, against the better judgment of sensible people, and so had lost his leg. It seems that all the rest – his story that the tree had his number and that he had the tree's number – was mere braggadocio.

It seems that he had watched Miss Mary's dinner party from his pasture. That he had not gone, claiming that Brown Girl was about to calf and always had a rough time, but made mighty fine calves. The old folks mutter that he was just plain jealous and useless, and had never dared to come to an agreement with Miss Mary when she was just Mary for the elders, when he was simply Theo, standing tall on two strong legs, tender only with his cattle. He hated Enoch's guts, they said, for getting her to give that dinner party for him as a sign of their engagement. At any rate, people all agree that it was no ordinary dinner party that Miss Mary gave.

Miss Mary was forty years old at the time, energetic, not pretty, but vivacious and strangely attractive. A joyful soul in a dispirited corner of God's earth, she was strong-willed and strong-bodied alike. She was not married, which everyone understood. But no details were ever offered regarding the substance of this understanding.

What was clear was that the Grove was home to simple country people; the men say little when the women are around, and the women toil and pray without ceasing.

Miss Mary was not like any of the women. The flounce of her skirt was no match for a bowed head, and though she worked as hard as any, her lips curled in a flare like that of her skirt. At forty she was not an old maid in anyone's estimation. Yet Candy, who was then pushing thirty and very active on the church guild, was already classified. In fact, the whole village was on the decline, and weddings and christenings were rare events.

It is no better today, yet my mother is not rejoicing at my impending betrothal.

Perhaps the decline in the population and the current exceptionality of ordinary events had been imported into the Grove along with the new pastor. From the beginning, he preached relentlessly about all manners of multiplication except the type that keeps a village from generating old fogies. His theology classified mirth as a sin. His High God brooked neither jokes nor revelry. He dwelt in such chilly heights that the ungodly, silent as mice, wondered how he would kindle the eternal furnace that was their promised portion and cup. Had the pastor's Almighty not frowned on science as man's pride and folly riding for a fall, He would have reconsidered His initial programming of humans. He would have approved the aseptic expedient of medical insemination to bypass the snares of the senses. Pragmatic, though, he approved the procedure for cattle, which neither lust nor laugh.

In the Grove of the latter days, only Miss Mary and the rare child laughed. At sixty-seven, she's still laughing, too. But on the night of the dinner party she had almost all of Howard's Grove working its jawbones in the most indecent ways; fêting the body and its joints with the soul – a soul that had nothing to with the pastor and his friend, I John, the Seer.

The village was pretty small in those days: five families in all, plus a dozen migrant field hands, among them the odd couple, one family, and all the rest single men. Mary, at twenty-five, had cajoled her father into building her a small cottage, two rooms and a porch, a little way from the family house, across the green; so she was both at home and on her own, working with her parents till they were too old for heavy chores, helping her Aunt Myra, her sisters and her brothers' wives, and looking to her own affairs, especially when work in the fields slackened.

Church for her was once a week while it was almost once a day for the other women, who liked to stick together.

"Near to church, far from God," she would say in a low chuckle.

But only to the older folks who had known other days and other ways, before the village in the Grove existed. Besides, God is certainly not partial to the little frame box that the pious people of the Grove have offered Him as a home since the foundation of the village.

The summer Big Enoch came to work as Aunt Myra's hired hand, Miss Mary's God was happily roaming the fragrant fields of Howard's Grove. Often, He bumped into Miss Mary, and always he smiled at her. Could she tell? She was all grace that summer. Even the good people of Howard's Grove, fully aware that all is vanity, noticed with some surprise that Mary was really quite pretty.

The large brown eyes of my namesake, Enoch, were not blind, nor was he weak. He was strong and fearless in the ordinary things of life, but to his mind these did not include women. With respect to them, he was not bold. Besides, Miss Mary was the old lady's niece and he was a stranger and a poor man. So, by day he captured visions of Miss Mary's ageless charm between his lashes; at night, as he lay on an old blanket spread over the warm hay of Aunt Myra's barn, he took them out, replaying them on the rosy screens of his closed eyelids till sleep stole him away. The next day, the living vision would walk the Grove, fragrant with the smells of ripening, a bounce in her steps, her skirt flouncing around her firm brown calves.

~~~~~

Many a week went by, the air warming, nature mellowing, the familiar summer breeze blowing down from the nearby hills, charged with the spicy spunk of cider wood. From the south, the sea breezes wafted in a cure of iodine. They brought back memories of the time before the new pastor, before Howard's Grove; memories of the old farms near the sea, near Howard's Cove, before the hurricane drove them further inland… Sniffing, the old people unscrewed their frowns, despite themselves, as recollections of the barn dances of the old days caught them by surprise in the act of tapping a foot, of shaking a head to once beloved rhythms, now forbidden in these latter days, rife with the smiling snares of folly and evil. It was a time of contradictory winds, that for sure, and who could stand unbending in such a change and not wonder how it would end, for the church, the Grove, and all the people?

~~~~~

It was in this season of ripening, swelling and reminiscence that the dinner party took place.

What words had passed between Miss Mary and her Enoch? Had they seen visions or dreamed dreams? Did Enoch, a stranger, know what it meant to be the special guest at the dinner party of a single woman? Did Miss Mary trick him and slip the knot around his unsuspecting neck before he could say 'Jackmandora!' or utter some other native spell to break the charm? How had she invited him? When? Where? No one knows. The fact is that she did. He, doubtlessly, accepted; and an uncommon festivity ensued, to the near peril of the souls of the Grovians.

D-day, quite unfittingly, was a Friday. A day of passions. Payday. The time of unspoken rendezvous for the young men, who invariably sneaked off to Howard's Cove, as long as the weather was nice or merely tolerable, until marriage put an end to their youth, its misdemeanours and wayward roaming. The Friday of Miss Mary's betrothal, they did not sneak off; they, too, were Miss Mary's guests.

I remember the dinner party as if I had been there. And so I have, oftentimes, in countless ways. Forcibly nowadays, as my relatives try to dissuade me from marrying Miss Mary's daughter, though never in so many words. Suddenly, Miss Mary stories are everywhere. Alone, I return repeatedly to this dinner party, turning it inside out like a glove. I have searched the hearts and souls of its protagonists and witnessed the sweet scenes of intimacy between Big Enoch and Miss Mary. The ripe moon had melted in tenderness above them and the tufted grass had tittered its complicity. The people of Howard's Grove, who were not there, paint this tryst in the crude and lurid tints of immorality.

Knowing these hidden scores, I smile like a fellow escaping to happy Howard's Cove on payday. I go there, too, often, for my research on marine life, but never at the weekend. At the weekend I return to Howard's Grove to see Awa, my light. We spend Friday nights conversing endlessly, plotting the future, deciphering the way out. When I take leave of Awa, I smile a secret smile – mounting from my loins, from my guts, from my heart – loving her more and more, swollen with anticipation, a trifle anxious.

It isn't easy to resist Howard's Grove, even when you don't love it; the surrounding gloom finds a chink and seeps in insidiously. When it does, I think back to Miss Mary and the first Enoch, to their honeymoon in the moonlit fields, before their wedding day, and strength flows back into me.

Of the private moments of Big Enoch and Miss Mary, of Awa's cherished beginning, I will say no more. Let them see and see, and remain blind; hear and hear, and not understand.

Let them invent scandals, ignoring the death in their doorway.

<p style="text-align:center">~~~~~</p>

To tell the truth, I too relish the dinner party stories. During the tellings, I love the Grove for a while. I harbour a glimmer of hope. One story of Miss Mary's dinner party goes like this:

That ripe Friday morning of the high season saw Miss Mary humming, busy as a bee in her halter dress with a flared skirt festooned with a single row of ruffles. A blue dress. Blue as the summer sky. Printed with small white seagulls. They soared on Miss Mary's dress, as do the real ones by the sea, at balmy Howard's Cove. They flew like the fleecy clouds, carding their leisurely dreaming high above Howard's Grove. Miss Mary was all oneness and peace. If peace had a spring in its step. If peace could take flight at any minute and become joy.

Howard's Grove watched her with curious, wary eyes.

The dinner preparations took place under cover. None of the familiar smells of this household ritual could be detected. No fragrant fruit pudding. No rich aroma of baked ham, of roast, of a simmering stew. No tease of cherry pie. No sizzle of fried chicken. No whiff of ginger beer. The green before Miss Mary's cottage saw no long table draped in white. Instead, several small low tables were scattered here and there, covered in lemon-green cloth with turquoise lozenges. All except one seated between two guests and four. The tables were oddly set. No grandmother's china. No ornate glasses or fine silverware, but stoneware, ceramic and everyday cutlery. Squat drinking glasses of every conceivable colour! There were no flowers floating, sweet and demure, in crystal bowls. No floral centrepiece crowded the middle of the high table, and no high table, of course. Miss Mary, her chaperone, and Enoch, her fiancé and guest of honour, sat on the porch of the cottage. To be near to the kitchen, she explained cheerfully, calling attention to her culinary duties. Seated just below, her female kin sweated in open apprehension, fanning large bosoms.

Soon the guests were all in place. The fiancé, seated facing Miss Mary, sipped lemonade. The fiancée's chaperone, occupying the third seat of the table on the porch, was none other than Aunt Myra, Miss Mary's godmother. Enoch, my namesake, had cleaned up remarkably. He would have been gorgeous had it not been for the unusual proximity of the old lady. It left him awkward and dumbstruck. Miss Mary seemed not to notice her aunt's stern demeanour. After the first glass of port, scowls had mellowed into mere frowns. There were even suggestions of a smile, here and there, as Miss Mary thanked her guests for coming, explained the seating, and presented the meal.

The seating was wherever you liked. As for the dinner, everyone already knew that she did not cook. But the important thing was to come together to celebrate her union with Enoch. No, she did not cook in the usual sense of the word, which usually involves an oven at some stage, for a party. She had never had the patience, so all the dishes that she herself had made had been boiled, steamed or sautéed in strict observance of respected experts. They should be quite all right. The women folk buried their shame and the men folk their anxiety in much the same way: they refilled their glasses, but not with lemonade. This second round had them feeling ready for a revolution.

"Cut the chattin' and bring out the fare!" Old John commanded. And the guests to a man agreed; some slapping their thighs, others mopping their brows. So, Miss Mary brought out the fare.

For starters, she served spring rolls with shrimp sauce.

"Here's to the steaming," said Aunt Myra, with an almost imperceptible smile. It was due in part to nervous tension, in part to ignorance, coloured wholly by her admiration of Mary's personal variety of the family spunk. The first course was declared unusual, tentatively tested, then put away without a clear rating. Was it good or bad?

The translucent phalluses of Miss Mary's strange sausages fascinated me. They took me back to my younger self. I licked the bright sauce off my fingers. It reminded me of ... what exactly? My head on my mother's lap at noon on a warm day? The smell of my teen-aged brother's bed early in the morning?

I would sneak into my older brother, Abra's bed, and snuggle beside him. My father had taken to chasing me from my parent's bedroom, but on many a morning I still felt the need to nestle next to a familiar body. Abra's warm bed would remind me of the smell of the sea at Howard's Cove, and I would doze off again for a while.

Big Enoch said nothing about the spring rolls, but he smiled fondly at Miss Mary. He found her vegetable sausages witty, her sauce brilliant; subtly flavoured with herbs he could not quite identify.

Aunt Ama suspected that Mary had added ginger, which is not good for you at night. Makes you restless. Gives you heartburn. But, then again, the taste was not quite frank, not pronounced, and you never knew with Mary. As a child, she had slipped thyme into her mother's jar of rosemary to avoid a reprimand for accidentally breaking the jar of thyme. And what cause had she to be searching her mother's shelves, and such a high one, too? The old lady's indulgent smile was a compliment to a tiny sip of dry white wine, which had followed the port.

From the summer light sky, God smiled down on Howard's Grove. It was not in response to the pastor's slurred, incessant, "Yes Lord!" But, it was good to see the poor fellow loosen up.

In fact, the pastor was light years away from his favourite pursuit: mentally wooing the state of holiness that would lend power to his words so as to persuade the congregation to increase their offerings, believing *at long last on the promise of God to recompense forty-, sixty-, and a hundred-fold the generosity of his chosen flock.*

"Chosen flock," muttered the pastor to himself. He half-chuckled, imagining the goats on the last day – jumping and bucking and raising hell, until the blast of the last trump and their just deserts. Delighted, the holy man downed a hearty gulp to this merited chastisement as Miss Mary dashed in and out of the cottage, bringing out the main course: farm-fresh zucchini, new potatoes, steamed, seasoned with lemon, butter and herbs, an enormous platter heaped with generous slices of Leo's famous smoked ham, bought the day before at his store at the Howard's Cove, another garnished with sautéed chicken… Chilled fruit cups polished off the fare.

The food didn't look right; it didn't taste right. But it wasn't bad at all, and the wine was good and served in abundance. Before long, the pastor's gaze dissolved into silent stupor, and there was no one left to frown or scold, or so they thought.

Aunt Myra had developed a high, girlish laugh. Big Enoch was still a bit shy, but he was no longer intimidated. He looked handsome now, replete with quiet strength. And his lover's eyes grew wider and wider until you thought there would soon be room enough for Miss Mary to walk straight into them.

Then all hell broke loose. No one had seen Old John come and go. No one had noticed the conspiratorial tones and the heads held close together of the four old timers at his table in the shadows. But suddenly all eyes were turned in the direction of the brightly lighted porch where the four were tuning the instruments of a makeshift band with fife, fiddle, horn and cymbals.

Old John, the ringleader, spoke up.

"If I was any good at making speeches, I'd have proposed a fine toast to Miss Mary, here, to wish her and Enoch all the best. I ain't no good at that. But in the ole days, I was mighty handy with the fiddle. Me

and the other ole boys here, we wasn't partial to playin' some music and shakin' a leg. A joyful noise and some prancin' is mighty fine in the eyes of God. It's right there, black on white, in the Good Book. Old Man Bill used to say 'music is the food of love'. So let's get cooking!"

The band started to let off steam, Aunt Myra called out the figures and the old folks were the first on their feet. They twirled and curtsied, bowed and shimmied as the pastor slept on, hearing the last trumpet sounding, watching the unsuspecting goats bounding and capering over hills and greens to their imminent doom.

"They don't know what's going to hit them!" chuckled the pastor in his sleep, the corners of his open mouth drooling, his breath reeking of fermented fruit-of-the-vine.

Soon the rhythm changed, it waxed slow and sentimental; young and old formed couples, wooed dreams or courted nostalgia, now smiling into a familiar face, now smiling up at the butter-yellow moon or at the bright stars of the summer sky. Miss Mary and her Enoch slipped away for the Promise Walk, in keeping with the custom, as the party drew to a close and the guests shuffled or drifted home, soused and happy.

At half past one in the morning, Aunt Ama found herself all alone at Miss Mary's house. Her sister, Myra had long since gone, tired but happy, quite unlike herself, forgetting her role as Mary's chaperone, who should be there to wish her goodnight when she came home from the Promise Walk. Imagine Myra playing the fool at her age!

Miss Mary's aunt, Ama, had not progressed beyond a smile all evening, and as the band started raising a rumpus, her face had retracted into a decided scowl. Aunt Ama cleared the tables, washed the glasses, and too tired to do more, put the plates and dishes to soak, knowing that Mary was quite capable of leaving them right there till the next morning.

Two o'clock. It was well past the bedtime of decent folks, but Mary was still out. How could she...! Three o'clock. She had not been raised like that! Aunt Ama fell from exhaustion onto Miss Mary's couch and slept there fitfully until five in the morning. But the bride-to-be was still not home at six, after the old lady's morning devotion. What in the world...? Aunt Ama, overcoming an uncomfortable fear, was about to raise the alarm when in walked Miss Mary, pleased as pie, calm as pumpkin. The Harlot!

"Oh, Auntie," Miss Mary said, "Up already? Enoch and I are going to church tomorrow for a public celebration of our marriage."

Aunt Ama gave no reply. She pulled herself up to her full five feet five and, brushing stiffly past Miss Mary, went away to her own house.

Miss Mary slept soundly until noon, then rose to repair the wreck of the night before, while her Enoch went off to sunny Howard's Cove to order a complete traditional wedding luncheon from Leo, who was also to provide the tables, the flowers and the decoration. A full catering order, he called it. The wedding took place on Sunday, as Miss Mary had said. It was followed by luncheon on the green by her cottage.

~~~~~~

Big Enoch enlarged the cottage and the old timers adorned it with latticework and carved columns for the new porch. Awa was born the following spring. Big Enoch "disappeared" six summers later. He just up and left; never to be seen again in Howard's Grove. Miss Mary offered no explanation. She continued to be quite herself, but left with Awa, two weeks out of every summer, for an unknown destination, and started to take her mail at the Cove. Awa, at birth was a lovely child, and unlike many, she waxed in grace and beauty as the years went by.

This year she is as fragrant as a rose bud unfurling, garden-sweet with a mystifying hint of something from another sphere. I call it musk. I am not sure why. This year, when the burnished leaves of an exhausted summer flutter to the earth, she shall be my bride.

I hope that my mother will bear up and take things with philosophy. At any rate, Awa and I will have no need to care for her frowning: between the two winds courting Howard's Grove, spicy cider wood and bracing iodine, we have chosen, without waiting for time to tell us what any fool can know.

I have already bought the land on which to build us a house at Howard's Cove. Awa will throw in her savings to make it pretty and snug. I've always liked it better by the sea.

I explained this to my mother's tight face and she uttered not a word; Nana didn't even try. She knows that I have made up my mind. Yet it makes me wonder when I watch her sitting there before me, still as a felled tree, and for all that the very picture of a woman battling with fate, wringing her hands.

I explained the pull of the sea to Awa's mother, Miss Mary, now a permanent resident of Howard's Cove, spending a mere two weeks at Howard's Grove, as a yearly visitor. She laughed, with her head thrown back, delighted.

"Well ain't you smart, Enoch, to prefer the sea," she chuckled.

"It's where it all began; there's no better place to start afresh! Besides, your Awa takes to the sea like a fish! And I ain't wishing you no happiness either!" Miss Mary laughed again.

"Smart as you are, you two might just start thinking that life is a *free* bed of roses!"

We laughed together, our throats to the sky.

I am a gardener, and Miss Mary knows it. I also fish. We have no need for wishing. Awa and I know how to work beauty and fragrance out of the earth, as the witness of our four hands can tell. There'll be good food aplenty for the cook we'll hire.

Maybe it's all that iodine in the air at the Cove that's making us giddy, but Awa and I agree that Big Enoch and Miss Mary have a thing or two to teach us about life.

Guess what, we're willing to learn.

December Evenings

That December afternoon was drawing to a close when I pushed the green wrought-iron gate and entered Aya's garden. It is separated into two almost equal halves by a pathway of round slabs leading up to the house. Aya's house sits at the very end of the garden, set way back from the quiet street that doesn't have a name, only a number: Street 106.

I had been feeling in my body the strange anticipation mixed with anxiety that still rises in me on December evenings. The bite of the harmattan wind, like an alluring but imprecise promise, had made me keen and sharp, with erratic swings, from joy to brooding sorrow.

That whole day, the wind had been laden with the 'silent devils' as my father called the sources from which my bad moods sprang. They had taken hold of me. And when they did I couldn't stand myself and no one, except Aya, tolerated the hostile silences that would possess me.

I was young and not carefree and only Aya seemed to find me normal.

"December is a strange month," I thought as I walked that afternoon up to Aya's house, my steps uneven on the large pebbles set into the round cement slabs of the pathway. Very impractical, that walkway, so unlike Aya.

I was almost on the doorstep before I caught sight of her and smiled.

A beautiful sixty-year-old woman was looking out at me from behind the slightly parted curtains of French windows. It was my grandmother, Aya. She had not gone on retirement and had

managed to get yet another promotion and a flex time arrangement
in the bargain. She had succeeded after many trials in having the
best of her desired worlds.

I had never called her 'Granny' or 'Grandma' for she found it
ridiculous. Didn't everyone have a name? She stepped aside to let
me in. Her eyelashes were painted with the electric-blue eye shadow
that was now in fashion. It made her look like a happy owl as she
smiled at me. But she did not touch me, said nothing at first, sat
down, patted a seat beside her, put a grey-blue Ghanaian porcelain
cup and saucer before me, and pointed to the teapot with her chin.
The teapot, swaddled in the English manner, made me smile.

Good old Aya! A philosopher and a joker, gay and moody; she
is all that. I looked at her, seated in her armchair, in her red, burnt
orange, cream and blue living room. Among her pottery, wood-
work, tapestries, calligraphies, and paintings; a judicious selection;
each piece with its own story: the story of a friendship, a journey, an
unpretentious patronage of young talents elected in keeping with
her own criteria. There was also a collection of pipes belonging to
her husband, who is not my grandfather. I do not take to him, and
prefer to visit when he is out. Aya doesn't seem to mind. "Now, I
have you all to myself, Missy," is what she says with a wink.

Aya had not always been my grandmother's forename. On the
eighth day of her birth, the crowd assembled for the naming ceremony had implored God's blessings on Nana Aziza. She had tolerated this name, according to my mother, until she was twenty-three.
A year after her Master's degree in law and finance, she had applied
for a legal change of her first name. My mother was not yet born.
My grandfather, Aya's first husband, had seen this as a bad sign (you
just don't get up one day and decide to be someone else): from the
day she had gone to the Family Court to submit her notarized name

change application, and before the judge's decision, she had refused to be Nana Aziza for anyone.

She claimed that the name Nana Aziza belonged to her father and his past; that it was holding her back. Nana was his grandmother whose only claim to posterity had been her two beautiful side braids adorned with brass coins and tales of her incredible millet fritters. As for Aziza, she had observed to Leïla (whose name she loved), who had been her roommate during the year that she had spent at the Cité Sarraounia Students' Hostel, who knows where her father had met Aziza? In what alley in Fez or in what courtyard of the old quarters of Bordeaux (For he had studied in both these towns and had loved the places of the 'real people'.)? In what movie? In what song or dream? Why Aziza? It was an impossible name to wear. Her father, who was no romantic as far as she could tell from her family life, should have chosen better. The name would not do. Hence the legal self-baptism and the new name whose meaning she never discussed with anyone.

"My name is Aya," is all that she would say in a level voice.

I loved the story from the very first time I heard it. I loved the simple finality of it.

I go to Aya's, often. I go to her always when life gets misty and I cannot see my way, or doubt that there is one. I go to her house, to her stories. I listen. I take her in. Especially in December. And on that particular evening, I needed to be near her.

While Aya served tea, I looked at her. I checked out her nails, lacquered a silvery white, very trendy, her eyes circled in blue, clearly not a look for an old woman. I gazed at Aya, sitting there, like I used to look at pictures of her and Hadjia Mairam when I was little, Aya and Hadjia Mairam in their dresses and hairstyles from the sixties, collarless, sleeveless dresses, with their knees exposed, posing besides their husbands, our old grandfathers (who now wear only boubous and soft leather babouches) in their Sunday best, with bushy afros, clean-shaven faces, Western suits and two-toned shoes. I still can't believe my eyes when it comes to the old people. But with Aya, it's different.

Despite my grandmother's indulgence, I started to feel a bit ashamed of staring so much. I am really not indiscreet by nature, but there is something slow and physical about my glance. It settles long and heavy, like a thing with a life of its own, and had begun to trigger misunderstandings with the opposite sex.

I decided to talk so that I would stare less.

"You are in great shape Aya." My words stumbled out, sounding fake and vaguely mocking. She noticed; I could tell, but she said nothing. I wanted to make her talk. About herself, about something, anything. My eyes roamed the room, searching for a pretext. No, not the albums of photographs that I had flipped through or studied, repeatedly, throughout the years...

Then, suddenly, I hit on it. That bow bereaved of its violin, in the home of my grandmother who did not play. That permanent decoration of her writing table where she did not write was strange, to say the least. I remember, when I was a little girl, seeing my grandmother with that thing in her hand. She would shake it at me, somewhat like a switch when, dying of curiosity, I would press her for an explanation. She would shake it at me gently and then grow still. Very still and suddenly absent.

I said nothing more. I stared at the bow with all my might, hoping that Aya would remember my old curiosity, that I would not have to say anything.

She caught my concentrated gaze. Her mischievous smile mocked me. Her face took on the expression of a woman facing a man who thought he was smart, soliciting without soliciting, reserving the ploy of the mistake in case of refusal: "What on earth made you think that I...?" And she, the woman, even smarter, noticing nothing, keeping up the banal tone of conversation, her face oblivious of any such thought or undertone, unsullied as the first dew of morning. Innocent. Anyway, her eyes were shining so, with such freshness, that I smiled again.

Now, at last, my smile was bold and free. And Aya spoke:

"Ever since I was young, I have had this philosophy: never refuse the gifts that life offers you. It had seemed to me, then, that this *never* should be boundless. The coyness of waiting, indecision: what a waste! Life is so short! This philosophy has gotten me into a spot or two of trouble. But it's ok. As my friend Mimi would say: 'today, my shining face is that of a woman passing through, who has eaten life with a relish'".

"Mimi is something else! I still have good teeth, too!" Aya mused.

She is proud of her teeth.

"And they haven't been idle, my dear! You find that funny? You wouldn't think, to look at me: now there's a woman who has eaten life?"

I wondered whether she was talking to me or to herself. I wondered what I had come for, really. But I was so totally present and receptive that evening that I can make it all come back whenever I want.

"Well, what do you see?" she asked, looking me in the eye, prodding. I did not answer. I did not want to interrupt her. I did not want to think about anything. I was contented to listen to Aya. I didn't have to believe her.

"Sometimes I hear your friends saying 'behind my back', 'your grandmother is a beautiful old woman; incredibly well preserved'. 'Preserved'! Like a shiny can of old beans, perhaps? Young people are so arrogant!"

But she turned inwards again and added softly, "It's ignorance, really."

And she smiled.

I turned a worried glance in her direction; I faced her fully with innocent eyes. "Not me, Aya," my eyes pleaded.

"I am not saying that for you," she said.

"I am rambling. What interests you is that violin bow. You know, the mysterious musician who owned it never really needed it at all! I have had that bow for forty years now. It was two years before your mother was born. Forty full years, but I still remember the afternoon I spent with him at the Boeuf Musicien Café.

———〜〜〜———

"The restaurant was an odd little hole in the wall with this atmosphere. The cool air gave you the impression of being in a cellar. The place was enclosed, but vibrant, inhabited; a dusky place, dotted here and there with yellow spots of light that shone out from small niches carved into the stone. Walls with a finish like pink-veined granite, when you got closer. Rough and precious, you wanted to run your hand over it.

This restaurant was a place for regular clients. You saw that as soon as you went inside. And only the rare passers-by going about their business in this part of town spared a second glance for that dark doorway.

The name of the restaurant was written in fading black letters, looping above the heavy door. It stood ajar. Was hidden by a low awning when it was closed – I noticed that only afterwards. It was quiet inside, no loud sound of laughter; but the calm did not prevent a sense of fun, as you and your friends would say. A sense of excitement that had nothing to do with the lighting or with anything else I could put my finger on. As I said, there was just this atmosphere.

The menu was posted on a tiny blackboard. You had to get close to make out what it offered in slanting letters that looped freely, rounded at the base, formed by the same hand that had painted the sign above the door. The miniature blackboard listed a variety of simple, classic dishes, some reinterpreted by the chef.

That day's specialty was posted apart: Boeuf musicien.

"Now, that's a very rare suggestion from the chef," the waiter said, answering the query on my face.

"And it is not a dish for everyone."

His lips formed these words delectably, with the almost snotty discretion of the initiated standing on the invisible line cordoning off a sacred space. He leaned towards me, speaking close to my face, pronouncing words that seemed to cost him. The muscles of his face moved like punctuation marks.

"It is not possible... not for every and anyone. It is not a common offering. Not even here."

Having said this, he straightened his bust and righted his slender figure like a whispered exclamation. The space between us returned. Even today I can still smell his perfume – a faint blend of spider lilies and damp undergrowth.

"I am not a regular." At this thought, a flash of anxiety overcame me. I turned my head towards the door, in a quick glance, but the night-blue curtain was now drawn between the door and the world outside, where life scurried with muffled steps along the dusty sidewalk.

The waiter took me by the hand. I returned, back inside the Boeuf Musicien Café. He was smiling at me now. Humbled, I raised my eyes to his face, unable to return his smile.

For some reason, I have been elected.

"Boeuf musicien...," I murmured feebly. There is worry in my voice, and a vague sense of pride.

"So there is beef in this specialty," I said.

"But the musician part..."

I was not playing the demanding customer; to tell the truth, I was out of my depth. I was trying to keep my countenance.

"It's part of the special," the waiter said, making a concession.

I refused to let him have his way. I tried to stand my ground.

"Yes, I can imagine," I said. "But what about...?"

My query was a modest response to his professional, almost authoritarian, tone.

"Accompanied by baby vegetables in a light sauce, with a sprinkling of crushed nuts, freshly grilled... and a musician," he answered.

He continued, insistent, "I would advise Madam to sample it: it is out of this world. And the braised beef in its juices is succulent. A pure delight."

A firm statement. A brief downward flutter of the eyelids. Devotional.

I couldn't believe it. Is this really an offer? And if so, what kind? My stomach grew cold and there was a lump in my throat.

"The musician...?" I stuttered, as long as he doesn't think that I... But he answered, without turning a hair.

"He is at the height of inspiration; he has been meditating for the last seven days in the company of his instrument."

"His instrument...?"

Dazed, I repeated the word like an idiot, in a tiny sliver of a voice. Why doesn't he put things clearly? The sauce for the vegetable seemed totally improbable.

"A violin, Madam, like they used to make them in the day!"

And now he was talking with his body, getting impatient.

"Say yes."

A frail figure had appeared by the waiter's side.

"This way, follow me. Our meal is served."

How did I get into this? How had they enticed me? Was that what it was? Why had I turned my head towards their dark doorway that afternoon as I walked down the street; a street like any other street, a stone's throw away from the town centre?

A few steps away, outside this cellar where languor overwhelmed you, the sun was still shining, *brutally,* complained a voice inside me. The sun was still shining, *normally*, with a safe respectable glare and the cars were talking to each other in the poor language of strident honking.

But I could not moor myself to the cries of the cars in the street. I could hardly hear them. Here, it was impossible to believe that the street was merely a few feet away. I could not imagine myself outside, in sunlight, in the noise and bustle of the city.

The man, no doubt the musician, so thin he seemed frail, took me by the hand and led me to a small shadowy room specked with tiny lights fitted into the ceiling. When he held me, I noticed that his grasp was firm. The room was furnished with a divan. Next to it, the meal was served on a low table. Through a mist of anxiety I made out a carafe of water, with no glasses. There was no cutlery either.

～～～

Aya was so absorbed that I tried to breathe lightly. I did not want to disturb this story rising from the past. I may be ignorant, but am even more curious. Aya's head was turned to one side; one full brown cheek was all I could see of her face. But my fear had alerted her. She turned slowly towards me, coming back.

"My child, I shouldn't tell you the rest of this story. But nowadays, you all know everything so soon..."

She looked away again, fixing the line of a horizon that I could not see, where I could not follow her. She sent me snapshots, from far away. She an astronaut in orbit and I watching on television.

"That man had me eating out of his hand."

She selected snapshots, deciding which ones to show me.

"He mothered me. Took a little of this and that. Put it in my mouth. I can't quite remember the taste of the food. He was feeding me in no special order. I accepted whatever he gave me, asking no questions. But I remember his hands. I ate them. His fine fingers tasted of nuts and gravy and... I don't know... Did I say that his grip was firm? His fingers were fine and supple. I remember. The skin did not wrinkle at the joints. It was flexible, elastic. Under the skin, I could feel the ligaments and bones with my teeth. I went on and on. I gnawed and licked, tirelessly eating the hands of a man that I didn't know. I would recognize those hands anywhere..."

My smile mocked her when she said that. Forty years had passed over those hands! In the event that they were still... But knowing that her feelers were out, I took no risks. She was still wrapped up in hungry caresses, giving, receiving. I could sense it. Good God, Aya! Don't tell me....

But, still, I listened.

"His violin was on the divan, lying between us like a guardian angel. But it could do nothing to quell the wave that was rising inside me. Was it fear? I don't know, but making a weak effort to control whatever it was, I asked for the musical accompaniment promised on the special menu.

So he started playing. I sang, inventing words to the music he was playing. I lost all sense of place and time. What had they given us to eat? When I emerged, I was under the impression that he was still playing, and my voice, moistened, floated back to me as from afar. Was I tipsy? Crying? He played on, but it was over my body, now surrendered, that the bow of the violin was running. He gave me goose bumps. I paid him back. We drank nothing. No. But his mouth..."

I was sure that Aya was gone now, forgetting me, imbibed in her memory.

"He had this way of kissing...".

She turned over that picture, put it aside, and substituted a joke.

"You wouldn't think so, to look at me, but I know a lot about kissing," she said.

She had returned, was suddenly quite close. Was she teasing me?

"Had I gone further with all the boys I kissed, your grandfather would not have..."

She looked away again, went back to sorting her photographs. From time to time she held one out to me, from a distance.

"I will not lie to you, little mother (she liked to call me that), by the end of that meal, we were no longer strangers to each other.

Night was falling. It was December, when night comes early. I had left home in the middle of the afternoon, to air out my troubles. The air had begun to sting near three o'clock. It had been windy, full of spirits, according to the elders, and now it was almost six o'clock. It was time to part the blue-black curtains and return home.

I did not know how I got home, on those legs that were no longer mine. Outside, the air was nippy. A veil of dreams fluttered between the town and me. Harried taxi drivers honked their horns, surprised to see a young woman, staggering, at dusk, playing with life, courting death.

As I walked up the street perpendicular to ours, the veil that had enveloped me lifted slightly. In the yard of an abandoned house, stood a gigantic Gao thorn tree where hundreds of cattle egrets nested, filling the air with their cries and the powerful aroma of guano. The tree was primeval and splendid and the egrets, palpitating like white flowers, renewed it all day long with their fluttering.

As I reached to open my gate, his voice came back to me. I replayed our last exchange like an actress viewing a scene in which she had played a minor role, a bit part. At the end, as he was taking leave of me, in the doorway, his violin and bow in his hand, a fit of folly came over me. I wanted to hold on to the dream. I was too young to understand. I wanted him to play me forever.

"Let go of that violin!" I said.

I did not finish my thought. I dared not, but thought it nonetheless.

Holding out his beautiful hands towards me (towards the door?) he answered.

"Don't hold your breath!"

But he smiled and gave me the bow.

So that was it?

Aya was back, alert, silent, her eyes shining, her pictures stashed away.

No doubt, my grandmother saw through me that evening with her elder's eyes that pierce through the thickest walls. She had decided to open that door of her life to me, just a crack. But she said no more. She simply sat there facing me, the skin still taut over her high cheekbones, her moist lips drawn into two still lines. She got up slowly and drew the curtains on the garden that was sinking into the night. I got the signal. It was time for me to go.

I did not find myself after that December encounter with Aya, but something must have taken root that day in the darkness inside me. I am not a philosopher like Aya – for me, the muddle of life settles down from time to time, and then I see clearly for a while until it gets murky again – but I love stories. I listen intently. I don't believe everything, but I keep going back to Aya's, throughout the years, always when she is alone.

It took time, a lot of time, for me to make a way and a name. I did not marry early like Aya, or my mother. After many years, I met the man with whom I now play duets – a metaphor merely, for Jean is not musical. But that's all right. I love his wit, his potter's hands, his cooking. He calms me down. It is I who proposed to him. At least I think so. It was a December night, in Bordeaux, on New Year's Eve.

I still go to Aya's when the mood takes me. Usually, she lets me arrange when. I have to travel to do so now. I had been thinking of calling her. I haven't been home in two years, although we make a decent living here and I am self-employed. It's the end of November. I want to see Aya. To hear her. But this time, it is Aya who calls me first. Her voice is vibrant and I imagine the light in her eyes. She brushes my worry away with a laugh.

"I have a brand new project, Missy! And I need your advice. When can you come? It's not a matter we can settle over the phone."

"God, Aya! You're a witch!" I say.

"I was about to call you for that very reason. I mean, a holiday at home… I know better than to ask you for details at this point…" I add, fishing.

She doesn't bite, of course, but she is happy to know I'll be coming soon, for a whole month.

Aya rings off and I sit there holding the cordless phone in my hand.

My head spins happily with the novelty of Aya needing me.

Magda

Taking Magda to the Thyll for a two-week holiday was turning out to be a sad mistake. The mountains seem to make her mute and jumpy. Or maybe the climate is simply a pretext. But like her, mountains keep changing, so I'm hopeful. Especially since yesterday.

We hiked way up to the old cabin with its bed of coarse planks in which you could still see the signature of the tree. We took off the thick rough linen in which Marcel had kept the bed wrapped since he had made his final move down to the relative warmth of the Thyll and Magda and I snuggled into the musty down mattress, sneezing and tittering like children.

The bed had been Marcel's until the late sixties, when he used to spend a hundred days up there with the cattle, descending only once or twice. If supplies ran out, he would send a message down to the valley with the dog to say, "Out of bread" or something like that.

"They would send some," Marcel explained to me one purple evening during the Easter week of 1985.

"It wasn't like nowadays; we worked hard. We started young and stopped when the body gave up to weakness or death."

His strong mouth twisted slightly with something like nostalgia, for he was not weak, but his son wanted him to rest and enjoy filial generosity, and Marcel had been trying hard to oblige. Fifteen years later, when I returned, alone, he had joined the Association of the Friends of the Thyll and seemed busy and content with his new life in the valley. The Friends welcomed me with their quiet warmth for a weeklong stay. And now here I was again, with Magda.

I had not written to announce my marriage but Marcel, Jacqueline, Robert, Anne-Marie, and the other Friends took us in without reproach. I adore the mountain people here, who take to you on the spot or not at all, unlike the ones in our place, who watch you for years, wryly, before they decide. Happily, when Magda first met the Friends, her eyes shone with gentle warmth, answering theirs, and she was adopted.

People who don't know Magda find her arrogant. But that is exactly what drew me to her in the first place – the way she kept others at arms' length until she decided otherwise – if she decided otherwise. It's a good way to be when you are a woman.

We are mountain people, Magda and I. But her mountains in Rwanda are different from the rugged nooks to which my people fled, ascending up and away from the sea. Generations later, I still have relatives who nest high in the crags like rock crabs. They speak a peculiar dialect and find sweet sleep when, and only when, their beds butt the hip of a mountain.

My friend, Thomas, Marcel's son, was a mountain man, too. We had met as students at Sciences Po in Paris. We had spent a few Easters together in the Thyll – never a Christmas – despite Thomas's embellishments on the virtues of sharp clean air and pure white mountains.

Marcel is an old man now, measuring the valley with careful strides. Thomas and I keep in touch. He's a big-time professor in Australia, sending fat quarterly remittances to his dad's old bank account in Chambéry. And here I am, in the Alps with Magda, trying to crack her shell. You'd think that was my scheme this summer – not resting from my job, where I spend nine months a year trying to hammer the rudiments of political science and constitutional law into the heads of kids who'd rather be government ministers or commercial traders with big houses and fast cars.

Recently, a spirit of contradiction made me want to see – to make – Magda open up. I thought a holiday in the mountains would do the trick. That's strange since I value Magda's reserve, her air of secrecy, her silence in public. Her restraint around others boosted the sense that I had access to a private place. But was that really true?

I used to think that Rwanda was the past. Magda lost all her family there in the genocide – the slaughter, she calls it – all save the scattered few who managed to flee to Burundi or Belgium. I eventually came to realize that Magda could never pluck the highlands of her childhood out of her heart (and why should she?), swear as she might that she'll never set foot there again.

But I've been thinking, too, that it's high time for her to spit it all out so we can move on. Time for her to voice the constant fear that dogged the flight to safety, to utter the unsalvageable loss, to name the congealed blood of Baba and Ma, of Edith and Ken and the twins, turning brown all over the burnished wood floors of the Blue Ranch, to face the unspeakable stench of dead bodies and the dank sliding of survivors down the side of the night, fleeing like animals from a bush fire. I want to hear her tell the story of survivors like herself, torn by the same terror, dreading the present and the future, with a fear inseparable from hope.

They had learned to descend into a nook of silence. I knew this. I knew why Magda was so quiet. But this knowledge was not her gift to me. I cherished the hope that one day she would offer me in words that I could comprehend the commotion that spilled from her at nights, in her mother tongue, escaping through the cracks of sleep. Magda speaks in her sleep, relentlessly, no matter where we are. And it was the same here, in the Thyll.

I thought it best to challenge her outright. Still, I did so taking every precaution, explaining that I needed to know her better, pleading hunger for the trove of her missing years, conceding that she would be free to share her story in her way, in her own sweet time.

Magda took me at my word. All good, she accepted; she would tell me her story. But was it all right if she let it come naturally. However. Whenever. If she felt it coming, could she just say, "I am going to tell you"? Would that be okay?

It was.

We had made a deal.

But for a whole week, Magda uttered not a word; she made absolutely no effort to keep her promise. She was never going to change. I shouldn't have gone there. I decided to forget it.

But a week later, when the mist lifted, we went out for a long walk. It was a blue day. Sparkling, sharp and clear. Magda suggested we pause to picnic near a stream that gurgled down the mountain. Although we had bottled water, she stooped to suck directly from the stream. Removing her Danner Mountain Lights, Magda plunged her feet into the icy flow with squeals of shock and delight. We enjoyed a simple lunch of Reblochon cheese on rye bread, washed down with a bottle of fruity Pinot gris.

I had not felt better in ages. I confess that I do too much – what with teaching and research, community outreach and the cares of an extended family – and holidays have never been on my agenda. Doing nothing makes me nervous; schemes carefully crafted to ensure that 'everybody has fun' depress me, much to Magda's distress. But, here I was kicking back and thinking to myself that she was right again.

The hike had done me good. Stretching out on the light blanket we had carried, I watched Magda take her now wrinkled feet out of the water.

"It isn't so cold once you get used to it," she said, smiling.

But she seemed tense. Turning on me the eyes of a child about to be whipped, she mumbled, "I am going to tell you..."

I had renounced access to her secrets after long days of waiting. But now, curious and annoyed, I was forced to listen. I was thinking, "So here we go..."

"One Sunday morning," Magda began, "when I was still in Brussels, I was torn from sleep at an ungodly hour with the sensation of a fist gripping my insides. I had been there before – same shock, same bile in my throat, identical recurring dream. But that Sunday morning I understood the dream better than I had ever understood anything since the slaughter.

"Do you know that fright that kicks you awake in the middle of the night, more potent than any daytime feeling, stronger than the fears of wartime? Can you recall what it feels like when you wake up from a dream sure that something good is going to happen? Well, it's like that, going back to the past, then returning; it's electrical and chaotic. The little forked branches of the soul freak out till you no longer have a body and you're floating in the clouds. The sky's blue and the air's past crisp but you're not shivering. You're excited and calm, all at once. You're up there, with no body to pin you down, and, hell, it feels good! Your beloved daytime body is gone and you're okay.

"Isn't that crazy? The solution was there, all along – no body, new mobility and the knowledge of things. You let loose and rise up in the air. It is teeming, sharp and clear, with no glare of sun. The sun is for the happiness of the body, and you don't have one.

"I like this dream when I awake at the right time, after the ascension; not when all my cells are freaking out. It's definitely better than dreams of Fridays at the Ranch after Baba's cronies had drunk the cellar dry, leaving us to face the fire. Baba's ranting had been our catastrophe before the war. Can you imagine?

"Maybe we should get a move on, it's getting chilly," Magda ended.

That was it. She had finished telling me her story for the moment. But what on earth had she revealed?

It rained the next day, an insistent shower, thin and grey. We stayed inside. By eleven o'clock, our stomachs were growling. Magda got soup going, a ham hock, leeks, potatoes and herbs. Not precisely summer fare, but hearty and filling. It cooked all day, simmering high over the little fire that we had lit mainly for the pleasure, for we could have cooked on the gas range. We swallowed down bowl after bowl of hot soup, sinking into the crackle of the fire and the torpor of hibernation. The people in the Thyll probably observe Caribbean rules of courtesy, for no visitor disturbed our peace.

Spooned and distant, lost in our own worlds, Magda and I gazed endlessly into the fire. Her voice, like the rattle of a pot in a quiet room, jarred me back into my skin. It was hot and moist against hers.

"I am going to tell you," Magda whispered.

"I had sworn that I was never going to set foot into that house again. My anger had nursed on years of pain. My dad's favourite phrase on a drunken Friday night used to be, 'Bunch of bloodsuckers, get the fuck out of my house!' His cursing would send Edith, Ken and the twins whimpering off to the neighbours and I would stay with Ma, for protection. I don't know whose."

"Sometimes Baba wouldn't relent; Friday's frothing vehemence would extend into Saturday and Ma, obeying the pounding order to leave, would hoist bundle after bundle onto her large head and move down the road to her mother's abode, forcing the old lady to abandon her large airy kitchen to house what she defined as her daughter's pride."

"One Saturday, Ma decided that that was that; she was never going back, no matter how many weeks of Mondays Baba came to beg, 'Woman have a heart and help me save the family. Business is bad when you're not at the ranch'.

"Yet Ma had a heart. She visited him, overnighting sometimes on a Saturday (was this some kind of an anniversary?). Baba often came to eat with us despite our grandmother's scowl. On weekdays, Ken, Edith, the twins (always together, when they were old enough) and I, took turns sleeping at the ranch. On weekdays, Baba, who never remembered the torments of Friday nights, was another man, kind and witty.

"But one Friday, when I was fourteen or fifteen, he pissed me off. I can't recall why I was there on a Friday. It might have been during the six-month reprieve when Baba stopped his weekend drinking. Ma almost went back to live with him, but the old lady, who had weighed the pros and cons of six extra heads under her roof, had convinced Ma to extend the period of observation. It might have been the year when I was crazy about Eric Rusesabagina, the son of a neighbouring small farmer. Father and son would come to help Baba at the ranch. At seventeen, Eric's thick body and broad smile made the skinny ranchers' sons look like wimps. I fell for his manly charms with no opposition from anyone. Maybe Baba's Friday stupors had given us the chance to chat and kiss past Ma's eleven o'clock Friday night curfews. Maybe I had stumbled in light-headed and weak from a week's fatigue, and from hours of kissing Eric, to find Baba awake and angry. Whatever it was, Baba started up about his house again and this time it shocked the hell out of me. Maybe Eric had been building me houses on the moon or maybe I was growing up, determined never to resemble my mother. It was too late to go back to the old lady's house so, stiff with anger, I spent what I decided was my last night under my father's roof. It was a tough decision. I loved Baba and was his favourite, but I stuck to my guns. I continued to visit but never stayed the night, despite the hurt of his pleading.

"Last night, I dreamt that I spent the entire night in Baba's house. The source of the dream was purely intestinal. Indigestion gives you nightmares. The enzymes were doing overtime to break down the armour of oil that had formed around the golden French fries and spicy tomato sauce of my dinner. Inside my stomach, the red-tinged potatoes had morphed into a smelly, pasty avatar. The tiny workers of digestion were forcing my voracity to have some bodily use. They were drawing from the pleasure of the senses a meaning larger than the stomach or the brain, larger than you or me.

"If we listen, we can hear our bodies talking to us; telling us about people and the cosmos, about now and eternity. There you are, in the lap of the night, sleeping, while eternity knits its web and your head foresees a future of bones. It's a skull, a small cup of life, brimming its offerings through fearless openings.

"You wake up in the night, and you are not afraid. You think about your skull stripped of skin, muscles, and nerves, smiling in the mirror, loving itself, talking without a sound. Or singing. Or buried. You wonder if one day, the hand of a seeker will unearth it accidentally and place it on a rock in a gentle wind. Maybe, tickled, the orifices will chortle to the sky like children in the spring, or lovers. Or sing a new song, soft and penetrating, full of simple prophecies.

"I fell asleep hearing no voice, weighted on the trip down by a full stomach, not at all keen. One nasty lurch, like a plane suddenly falling, and I was off to oblivion, happy to escape from everything, the present, the past, and life itself. For a cycle of nine hours, I no longer existed. The playwright who had created my character endlessly saved and eliminated me each night when he wrote 'Magda exits'.

"A lurch, then a drop into the cave, and I become a yellow chick beneath the belly of a dark hen, safe, in charge of nothing. Dreaming.

"In my dream, I saw my father and my mother together. I wasn't keen on seeing either of them. But the night belongs to the dead. They sigh and move about while the helpless living sleep. The world turns upside down. I dislike these dreams of my parents. They are always so disapproving and judgmental. Who needs that?"

~~~

Who was she kidding? Throughout Magda's story, I couldn't keep still, could barely help yawning. In another place, at another time I might have tried to understand. But what was there to understand?

"Good God, Magda!" I blurted, "What the hell do you mean?"

A moment later, deflated or mollifying, I added, "Okay, let's go to bed."

When she turned to face me, I saw that she was crying.

On a mild Friday afternoon a week later, we were outside sitting on the grass trying out the prototype of a puzzle featuring the Thyll as it was in about 1900. The puzzle was easy, some three hundred pieces, and thanks to Magda we finished it soon enough to take a walk before a turn in the weather. We came back starving, in time for the Friday night soup at Robert's.

The evening went well until around eleven o'clock when the first polite yawns signalled that the elders were ready for bed. Empathetic, Magda joined the yawning. She had spent the morning packing our bags, as we were to leave the following day. She had made no further attempts to tell me her story and I had offered no encouragement. But now our stay was about to end. On impulse, I wanted to hear the rest of Magda's perplexing tale. But I dared not make such a request after last week's explosion. She needed no prompting, however. Apparently, she, too, needed closure.

"I am going to tell you," Magda began. And I held my breath.

"I love sleep and I don't love it. I love dreams, but sometimes they scare me. I love people, but not all the time. To be with them, you have to talk, and I prefer silence. It's nothing, really – no big secrets, nothing deep. Just a habit, a snug shell secreted around me.

"After the slaughter, I was a refugee in Belgium. My degree in psychology turned out to be a godsend. Giving conferences on survival earned me a good living. I managed not to talk about myself. Somehow, being an emblem of survival didn't suit me. I had money, but no one to send any to. No family to complain about. No luck, until I met you. Or you met me. Well, until we met. I took to you immediately. Was sure you'd give me space, that you'd wait..."

"Wait for what, Magda? And for how long? It's been five years!" My insistence surprised me, but it bore no trace of vehemence.

"Who knows? For a more... For a better... For the right time. For the courage to come out into the light," she faltered.

Her voice broke and my shell cracked wide open. Blood and certainty flowed out. I took Magda, her ghosts and my demons into my embrace. Silent, I rocked back and forth, accepting the whole mess.

That Saturday afternoon found us far from the mountains, on a smooth ride down to Cassis with our windows down. Magda's twists, glistening with oil, soft from the damp air, flew thickly around her face, mocking her attempts to control them, smudging her glasses.

And Magda greeted their defiance with a giggle of gold.

Into the Dark

Today I am dehydrated and unhappy. It doesn't take much to arrive at either condition, it seems, and the one is liable to lead to the other. Overall, my life is cresting; with rise and fall both inherent in the landscape. I am lured by the soaring green and blue of tree tops and sky, yet the waves suck and the valley pulls, and my senses veer up and swerve down; aspiring, fearing, surging, plunging. I tell myself that it's simply a matter of time, that before long I'll settle into the ecology of a higher ground. Still, today is a down day.

I rise and head for the bathroom, to retrieve a bottle of the ice-cold water I'd removed from the fridge, left out to warm up, and forgotten on the top of our tiny washer. I'm crossing the living room when I see Dog-the-lamentable settled as close as he can to the front door without actually getting inside – he knows it's not allowed.

He's there shedding ticks and oozing stench – happily, these days it's not blood dripping from his inflamed penis, smearing the tiles. I chase him back into the pissy end-of-August rain, a trickle, sluicing unpleasantly through a wash of hot sunlight. Dog-the-lamentable yields, slowly, unwillingly.

I do not venture out the door to threaten further as the veranda is damp and soiled with the wash-off from the roof and I do not want to dirty the brightly beaded Kenyan flip-flops I'm now wearing. The plain black rubber ones I had on earlier curl discarded by the coconut fibre doormat. I had worn my old black flip flops earlier to retrieve a ripe orange-sized lime that had fallen from the overhanging tree on the dirty veranda.

My limes are exceptional, huge, gorged with juice and flavour. I had only a dozen left on the tree. Eleven now. I'm saving them. I snatched this one up before anyone else could, even Mato. I did so, calling myself names in the process. Covetous, acquisitive, selfish, territorial, and more. With all these qualities, in thirty years' time, if I make it to my crabby neighbour's age, I'll be frightful, but she won't be there to see me triumph over her, "See, I've outmatched you, you old witch!"

I'm on a guilt trip. Because I refused to hand all my limes out one by one to Nabiya – I stopped at three. And because I refused to let Habi leave our house yesterday after the reception of Ana's bride price with a litre-and-half jug of juice made at home from said delicious limes. Plus mint from my garden, sugar infused with vanilla pods that Stephanie had bought for me in Paris, imported fresh pineapples, fresh ginger, my dead mother's recipe with my personal touch. No, I wasn't going to give the last remaining bottle of that elixir to Habi of all persons in return for her saying, "Ami, your drink is too good".

"No, Habi," I said, "Not you."

Tit for tat. She had been odious the last time I went to their house to see her aunt, not her – she's my junior and it wasn't as if she was sick or anything. Plus, she had been utterly raucous earlier in the evening, injecting uncalled for spite and noise into her cousins' tiff with Mato, as we sat waiting, way too long, for the suitor's people – men – to arrive.

Now, the day after, I wish I hadn't offended Habi. She isn't totally sane. I could have lied nicely: other guests were still there, chatting, we'd have to wait to see if there was any juice left when they were gone, but as she was leaving already....

I need to put a bit on my tongue. I ought to apologize to Habi, I think. But I doubt my readiness to go out of my way to do so.

Today's weather doesn't inspire charity.

I collect the warmed-up tap water. I head back to my desk, but not before having to chase Dog-the-lamentable off the veranda again.

Last night, my compassion finally depleted, after years of struggling on and off with Dog's various conditions, I approached Max – a vet, old Mrs. Crab's son and a 'little brother' – as he was leaving Ana's bride price ceremony, about putting Dog to sleep, but Max countered with a prescription for the animal's chronically sore ears, a repellent for the ticks and the flies and worm medicine to stop the wasting away.

There is nothing to prescribe against a dog's age or today's weather.

But is there a remedy against the murky currents that periodically pluck me down, making my journey longer and harder than it has to be? Or is the sorrow necessary too, part of a mysterious plan to which I would be wise to surrender; accepting all, even the threatening darkness?

If only I knew the answer. If only I were wise.

<hr />

Crude light is pouring in through the windows of my study, so I draw the thick maroon curtains that Vee made for me. I repel the light and the end-of-season sultriness, lest it dry up the water I'm trying to slosh back inside me. I care little for light, scenery, the chatter of birds, or the turmoil of Mrs. Crab's visiting grandchildren when I'm trying, waveringly, to get some work done, feebly opposing procrastination and sorrow.

"Today is a down day on the mountain-top," I sigh and reach for more water.

Outside my window two doves are fighting. Males, for sure, no coos of love. They batter each other, wing to wing and beak to flesh, vying for supremacy in their small kingdom.

Truth be told, I too favour guarded realms. I am no lover of grand expanses of land or sky. Strong light sears my eyes, which have no filter of natural lenses; it arrows straight into my skull. Sight-wise, I have no protective reflexes at all.

"Bad accommodation," the doctor explained when I was ten and already suffering from the glare.

I am a creature of the shadows, though not one of the night. As luck would have it, my body clock and my eyesight are out of sync. My body goes to roost at sundown and rouses before the east is pink, but I work best by day behind lowered blinds or drawn curtains. My favourite place in our house is my bedroom, lights dimmed of course, except my reading lamp, which must be bright for me to read comfortably. I control – or rather controlled – my environment in keeping with my handicap; my garden especially, with its secret nooks where a subdued sun warmed and dappled burrows of shade.

I am exiled from my garden now. Mato went and had the trees stripped behind my back – and his – while I was enjoying a rare summer vacation abroad, at my birth home. In place of the canopy of towering green that once conquered and sublimated the sunlight, thick dun pillars stand, almost nude, with a pitiful fuzz of green about their heads, beneath their armpits, at their crotch. Glare rules supreme, and worse will come. In March, if unmoved, the plants, which previously nestled in the shade that preexisted them, will parch and die.

"To travel is to return to strangers." A line from a poem that haunted me long before I had experience enough to perceive what might lie beneath the verse.

"Absence itself is like death," I think now, when, in the morning, I must muster the nerve to push open the bathroom shutters. When the sun slices the apples of my eyes.

See, you travel for two months only and return to find your sacred spaces trashed.

You have to guard the temple continually or face the consequences of absence.

While I rested in my far-away valley, enjoying the river that gurgled in the valley's lap, no little bird whistled, "Beware, the spoilers are thrashing the garden!"

I was plump and contented in the valley, on my own.

When it rained there my contentment escalated to beatitude. And it rained in the afternoons, invariably.

It was sheer bliss when the downpour bored deep into the night, the sky slashing down and the river roaring back until dawn forced a belated passage out of the gloom to reveal sparkling green trees, a thick brown river, and silvery-grey peace.

Not so here and now where Mrs. Crabb's grand-urchins squeal or whine, their voices echoing from various points of the neighbouring yard. Max, their dad, has not written the promised prescription for Dog-the-lamentable, and the power splutters on and off, disabling the fan and the internet.

~~~~

I'm dehydrated and unhappy, but I resist, sip by sip, studying temperance now, or rather, endurance. Rehydration takes time and it's too late for temperance, I should have practised that virtue last night. Thanks to the power cuts, the smelly, noisy, necessary generator, which is out of order, is finally missed. Five days after his promise, Hima, the man who is supposed to fix it is still coming.

I grimace a smile.

Max's children screech, cackle and hurl things that pound against the wall separating our yards, too skilful at chaos, they do not bump their little heads together. I sit at my desk regretting the old days, before women started laying little geniuses.

I'm not going to make it.

I'm not going over there to say anything. I am not their mother. She probably told them to go outside and play. They are obedient as well as smart, sadly.

Danger, children playing!

Watch out, woman boiling!

Caution, city-in-the-south floundering!

The power chips in and out and I refrain from fanning myself.

I try to get some work done. There are three draft chapters of Hachirou's dissertation in a folder on my desktop. I read the first, growing crosser at each line. Grimly, I repeat the same remarks, typed in red block capitals right inside his text. Doing this strikes me as invasive. I persevere, nevertheless, unwilling to create hundreds of comments per chapter.

Hachirou should not be attempting a PhD in cultural studies; he is no scholar: no humanities background, scant general knowledge, little understanding of what analysis requires, writing problems, huge ambition but always in a hurry. How does that tally with a dissertation on "The Wages of Migration: Irony and Desire in the Work Songs of Hausa Women from Tahoua, Niger"? How did I get into this? And how will Hachirou extricate himself from it? The thought of Balkissa's new chapters on "Identity on the Edge: Urban Youth Culture in Niamey and Zinder" lifts my spirits momentarily; Balkissa is thorough and brilliant. Ibrahim is pretty good, too. The others will manage. Hachirou, I don't know. Assessing these students makes me think of Mato, and my sky clouds over.

I leave my desk and go into the kitchen to heat up the leftover Turkish coffee that Mato made before leaving for Ouagadougou for a conference on peacekeeping and security in the Sahel. I pour the thick fragrant slush into a tiny, handle-less, cheap Ethiopian coffee cup and go out the back door to sip the strong brew in the shade. I don't want to think about Mato, now that he is gone. This is supposed to be my time to catch up and unwind, a combination Mato doesn't understand; but how could he? He doesn't have a husband to deal with. An ageing husband from another, different, world; one who is proud and good and dying.

The coffee gives me heartburn. This is why I want to cry, because of the pain that radiates out from my stomach, scorches my lungs, shoots up to my nose and mouth, making me sneeze and gag.

But I don't cry; I swallow bile and blow my nose on the sleeve of my caftan. I go back into the kitchen and rinse out my mouth with juice from a slice of lime, spitting directly into the kitchen sink, which is nasty, but I'm alone in the house.

I am not a cry-baby, so I don't cry. I don't, because if I start I'll not be able to stop and there is no one here to comfort me. I don't because I am strong, because I am the comforter, the dryer of tears, the firm bearer of bad tidings.

Because I can manage.

It's only a bit of heartburn, after all.

Walking Baby

"Abomey! Abomey!" I cried, homesick.

I took the child and the old bag and my umbrella (you never know) and some food for the child, in preparation for a long, long walk. The child was young, but no one of my acquaintance ever called it a baby. It seems that it had always talked, reached for my breasts, or yelled when provoked. Today, it was wearing a lovely pink knitted dress, and looked quite the picture of a sweet infant, resting on its mother's back.

So we went, chatting together of this and that. I threw my voice over my shoulder to the child, like a busy village woman pounding and breastfeeding without a break in her stride.

We stopped for the child to feed. It wanted no milk, now, but a nice ripe banana, it said, getting ready to yell. I peeled the banana and the child grabbed it and ate. We continued as before.

Soon, we sighted a fair and went in.

The fairground was on a slope further up the road. It was crowded and hot and the child's woollen dress was starting to draw remarks. It was too hot to have a little baby out in the sun, one woman observed, and in a woollen dress! Only a fool would do that.

I was no fool. I did not answer. As I could not beat them, I would join them. I would play along.

I threw the child to a woman her friends called Felicia, but it started to yell, so I retrieved it, put it on my back and tucked under the ends of the wrapper, fuming inside. The child, I knew, needed no carrying. Nonetheless, I slapped it to my back, and tucked under the ends of the wrapper. Tight. The little imp laughed. We laughed together.

"It's hot on that fairground!"

Those women again. It was the same heat everywhere. But here, the crowd was gay, and the music boomed, but those women were trouble. I decided to leave.

The music descended the slope behind me, thumping my back. The asphalt of the road beckoned, but I would dance before I went, I would dance right here at the foot of the slope, never mind those bitches. I cut a figure from the new dance craze, and got it right immediately. I tried it again and again, light and contented. Then I gasped; too light. Where was that child?

Turning, I saw it. It was lying a good yard away, motionless in its pink dress. When I approached and bent over, I saw that its eyes were almost closed. I took it up quickly, breathed into its mouth, then remembered. I had to breathe into its nose too: it was a child, after all.

I did what I had to till the child was revived. I was worried about internal injuries. The best thing was to go home.

The women from the fair crossed my path again, making loud comments, calling out to some men in a barbershop. Meanness was brewing, and it was a long walk home.

I went with the load on my mind, the baby's bag on my shoulder, the umbrella tucked under one arm, the baby grasped in the other (was it sleeping?). My legs pumped. I did not look back. I didn't want to find those people facing me when I turned to close the gate. They would claim to be thirsty for justice, although they didn't even know the child's name.

If worse came to worst, my people would hide the body and put the other twin on my back, with a wrapper around it, ends tucked tight.

Rosanna Goes Shopping

She is going shopping for the second time that day. She wonders why she's doing that again. She prefers to skip the details. She can guess why. Random thoughts assail her. She does not surrender. She does not let them flow at will like clouds in a summer sky. She challenges some, she dismisses others – well she tries – ignoring that others still elude her.

She strides forth, pounding the fine red dirt of what should be a pavement. She gets on with what must be done: shopping for food, raising healthy kids, imposing at home the cleanliness which is next to godliness.

She does not question the nature of this proximity. Next to as in what? A tangle of arms and legs in rumpled sheets? A 'good day to you!' shouted over a fence? Sullen chewing on the other side of the dinner table? What?

A new straw basket straddles her right arm like a statement. She does not know this. It would never enter her mind to announce: where I come from, we go shopping with a basket, not a plastic bag.

The basket, bought at a bargain in the parking lot of the only supermarket in town, is intricately woven. The natural paleness of its new straw circles two swirls of patterns in Sahelian red and green. The basket smells wonderful, like the earth, like a man, like a harvest evening.

Does a man smell wonderful? It depends. A man may exude fragrance, like a leather jacket coming in from winter rain – heavenly! Or smack of the funk of sleep and sweat squeezing through partially clogged pores. Or taste like seawater with a soupcon of lemon.

Well, that's a big chapter, men, needing a lot of imagination for the writing, if you see what I mean. She smiles, pulling inwards like a snail, leaving the shell of her body to the street. It is a taut body, not yet ripe, no longer slim. It is draped in a dress that clings at the top and swings around the calves.

Rosanna's legs measure the dusty sidewalk in great strides. She is back now, single and secure; her snail shell dissolves and she feels the power; the power to be present, there in the street. She swings her basket, posturing still, refractory, hurling energy out until she feels their eyes pecking. So much energy, they must think. They will not think 'so much imagination'.

They may be right.

Rosanna knows that she will never write anything, certainly not about men. They are such a tired subject. As over-worked as love, and she is not fond of love stories, although she knows she could write one a day. Could she? Her cousin, Hally, says it's a slave market, very badly paid, and they never put your real name on the cover, it's always some romantic invention instead. Samantha King. Rose Hawthorn. Tiffany Andersen. So what's the use? And, really, who could write stories, who could write *anything*, in the squalor of this excuse for a town? And how would Hally know?

She's never seen Hally reading and prefers to think that her cousin is so dumb she'd eat her name printed on a bulla cake and not even notice. Maybe she'd ask if there wasn't any cheese to go with the bulla. Or better yet, fat slices of creamy avocado, firm and tender. *Dry.* An important word, *dry*, if you know what I mean; as in rice cooked *dry*, or *dry* yellow yam; nice and *foody*. Rosanna revels in the terms of popular gastronomy from a place she doesn't miss, won't miss, ever; for she has chosen this place, this present. Ain't it, Hally?

Hally developed a greed for 'aint it' after a ten-day visit to her father's one-room flat in New York.

Yard, New York, perfect avocadoes and yams are distant planets best left alone.

Likewise, Rosanna knows that she will never write about men. Or love. Maybe one day she'll write about Hally. But that could be perilous. There's no love lost between her and Hally, so how would she control the story? It would poison her for sure. Wouldn't it? It would lap at her, suck her in, and she would yield to temptation and be odious.

Rosanna swings her lovely Sahelian basket; she ignores the rub, swallows up the dusty sidewalk with strong strides, and trills her name of the day. What's in a name? She has many. There's one that's a perfect fit for a day like this. A crazy day. A name which makes her children laugh. And worry.

They do not want their Mom to wake up saying, no, *singing*, "My name's Rosanna, Rosanna Bakwai!" never mind that she can't sing, that her name's not Rosanna or anything close; never mind that Bakwai isn't a name at all.

The children know this. They speak Hausa, as do their dad, and aunts and uncles; a great tribe, aware, every last one of them, that *bakwai* is a number, not a name; no need to think about it at all.

Rosanna's oldest child, Myrame is seven; it will be years and years before she discovers the follies, magic numbers and secret dreams of grown women. There's no rush, Myrame, no rush at all.

Swing, swing goes the basket, over Rosanna's sturdy arm. It's a Rosanna day today, a day for off-tune singing. She is singing now as the red dust kicked up by her sandals powders her feet and ankles, yearns for her shins and thighs and navel, for all of her; the shells of her ears, the fine hairs in her nostrils, the spaces between her teeth, the alveoli of her lungs.

"Come to the cab-a-ret, my friends, come to the ca-ba-reet!" she sings. Unable to sustain festive tunelessness, her voice dims into a seething hum, nursing banked fires. Her voice murmurs behind the bars of fastened lips, "This place is too much!" But it will not break. It will sing. It will hum. It will buzz back, and sting if nettled.

A cart man goes by. He glares at Rosanna. "Foreigner," he mutters. He's a serious man; he knows that only mad people, foreigners and peasants sing in the street. His cart strains beneath the burden of tumbling miscellanea, from powdered milk and toothpicks to cigarettes and soap powder. His lower back, shins and shoulders protest against the incline in the road as it mounts to Saga, while unburdened pedestrians and humming motor vehicles discern no change in grade.

"What is there to sing about?" the cart man frowns.

"Poor wretch!" he mutters in his native Zarma. But his body pleads for empathy.

"We are all God's slaves," his bunched muscles entreat.

The cart man grumbles winded assent. Grudgingly.

Engrossed in her singing and humming, Rosanna neither sees nor hears him. It has always been hard for her to make people out, but when she is present, really there, she can feel them. Now, she feels and sees the people and cars going by, ceremoniously dressed women entering the offices of the Sonidep Gas Company, self-important looking men wearing starched boubous and Saharan suits shiny from weekly pressing with heavy rustic irons filled with burning charcoal. She feels their readiness to snob an afternoon client for the heck of it. She has never been inside the Sonidep building. She knows only pockets of the town. She wants to know it better. To explore.

A footpath snakes between the Sonidep building and the neighbouring Christian Cemetery, coiling left and out of sight, into

shade. A path she has never taken. One that looks cool and inviting. She will take it now. She crosses the street. Brushing against
the important Sonidep office workers, she enters the shadows and
the odours that the occasional man or dog has left behind. The
smells give dog an edge over man; living or dead humans smell
more. Except when tightly sealed inside a tomb. Yet, Rosanna likes
cemeteries, the orderly kind you can find elsewhere. Not here, except maybe the Christian Cemetery, whose west walls she can now
touch by extending an arm. It has some order, but little scope and
no poetry.

Rosanna turns left into the shadows and makes a discovery.
Huddled behind the Sonidep building is another, new two-storey
building of roughly the same size, boasting a rotating doorway –
something she has never seen before in her seven years in this town.

"When did we get so modern?" she wonders.

"When did they build this?"

"Where was I?"

She has no answers. The shade and the newness unsettle her. Her
skin is tight and tense with its own excitement. She hugs the basket
to her chest, unsure of the fit between the straw basket, the chrome
door and herself. But there is ample room for her and her fat basket.
The chrome and glass door spins her into a gloomy hallway dotted
with dull neon globes. Rosanna follows the dim hallway with her
new basket that smells like straw and like a man, a certain kind of
man: the summer version of the leather-fragrant guy. It's a healthful
scent, like leaves in the evening sun. Through the door and across
the hall she goes. But she has lost her swing.

"So much walking today! Well, cheer up! It's good exercise."

Did she say that out loud? Luckily, there is nobody to hear, for
these people will certify you mad for a yes or a no, so long as you

say something, anything, in a language they do not speak, in a style that eludes them.

Rosanna's feet glide across the huge glossy squares of the too-cool empty hallway. The place smells …

It is then that she sees the *person*. She cannot believe her eyes. She rubs her free left hand, palm open, down her face. She looks again. He is still there. Wearing Suzanne's face. But she looks even paler than she used to, back in high school. Now, you could almost see through her greyish skin. Her hair is tucked back, concealed inside a bonnet, like someone trying to disguise. She looks like a man: her clothes, her eyebrows, her manner. A coarse man. Hairy. How could this be Suzanne? No; just a weirdo who, somehow, resembles her. Maybe it's the skin tone. No, the forehead. Nothing to do with Suzanne; just the same broad forehead, and thin-lipped mouth; perhaps the attitude as well. Domineering.

"Hey! You can't go through there. Stop! It's a private entrance!" the man shouts after her.

"Private, my eye!" Rosanna's glance sasses, unwavering. It's a match of the overbearing. Her energy returns. She does not turn back. She dashes for the door. The man follows, panting.

The man like Suzanne is heavy, like Suzanne. She hears him panting after her. There is time enough for her long legs to take her away from him, back into the light. But when she hits the end of the corridor, she understands.

The fat man was right, there's no exit here, only a stairway arching down and down and down. She dashes down the curving staircase. Her pursuer does not relent. He lurches forwards, puffing and cursing. But Rosanna can go no further. Two feet from the staircase, a heavy door blocks the final corridor. Rosanna is exhausted. She is not frightened. This is absurd. She doubles over, her face against the chrome handrail. It is cool against her sweaty face. Her breath is coming fast. She starts pulling inwards, like a snail into its shell, but catches herself in time. Not here. Not now.

The fat man is standing behind her on the stairs. She wants to turn around and face him, to thrust the basket between them like a huge belly, but there is nowhere to go.

The fat man's eyes are moist. Dilated. His fly is open. She can feel him; feel his energy. She does not fear him. She has no need to. The patient is not strong, but is in no danger of imminent death. The doctor has other matters to attend to; she has to go.

The fat man presses against her, like a patient feeding on sympathy. She remembers when he was Suzanne, a classmate for five consecutive years who never became a friend. Who used the word "excruciating" in grade seven. Who had migraines at age eleven. Rosanna lets this older Suzanne in drag lean against her. Then she feels it, hard against her back. Definitely not Suzanne.

She shuffles down, occupies the last stretch between the end of the staircase and the door. The way out is up, past the fat man. She will have to talk her way around him and the basket won't help.

She turns to face him, but when she lifts her gaze she sees it first. It is turgid and translucent. It makes her think of something hot associated with pain. A hot-water bottle?

"I was looking for a shortcut to the market," she says, meeting his gaze.

"I hope you don't mind," she angles.

He does not move.

His eyes are yellow and feverish.

Sleeping with the Doll

was busy looking for him and feeling very hot. It had been a while. A while away. And, strange enough, I always need him exactly when he isn't there. Or was it the novelty, the travelling, the leaving, the returning that had set me free, made me desire-full? The pleasure of a new landscape, a new scene that spoke to me and I would start to feel like kissing just about anyone on the mouth, multiples of anyone, regardless of age, sex or creed, beauty or grace. I would feel like kissing the grass, the rough bark of trees. I would blow kisses at the sky. Happiness has always spoken to my senses, and life has always drawn me by the lips, the mouth, the taste buds, the tongue. Life is food, drink, saliva, soft mucous linings, rush of taste-smells, textures broken down, mixed, chewed, synthesized, swallowed; something the mouth hankers after, watering synecdoche, the part witnessing for the whole. So here I was, back home, and very hot.

I went to his room. The door was slightly ajar. I could make out his features in the dimness, the curve of his arm hanging out of the bed, the way he held the hand that touched the floor. I thought of his satisfied smile during a good drink. A smile I hate, out of jealousy. I opened the little fridge he kept there to get light, but the door, patched with something, almost came off. I saw his face better and that reassured me. I needed reassurance for there was something strange about the room, about him. He is sensitive to the slightest noise at night, yet he had not heard me enter the room and move about.

I undressed with a shiver, thinking these thoughts, imagining how I'd wake him, how he'd react, how our lovemaking would be. I was getting into bed beside him, ready to move from thought to action, when a chilly voice emerging from the bedclothes arrested me.

"Were you thinking of joining us?"

I stuttered denial. Why on earth would I want to get into bed with my own husband? I would settle the matter with him. But before that, I needed to see my questioner.

It did not take long to find her. She young and slender. A delicate doll. At her side, he slept exhausted, exhaling little bubbles of breath, enjoying his sleep. I astounded and furious, caught her by the feet and turned her upside down. She was wearing white undies with blue trimmings.

"Still in pampers, I see!" is what I said, but her underwear confused and disarmed me. It was not her fault. He slept. She eyed me, cold and silent. I would have it out with him. Yelling, I slapped his sleeping face. He awoke. Stupid. Bewildered.

The room expanded to the size of a small assembly hall. People poured in, normal people, no Lilliputians; no one who resembled my miniature rival. Their arrival and movement distracted me and I returned to the problem of the duo, one had disappeared.

But I knew where to find him. I was through with making scandals. We were going to settle the matter reasonably. I wanted an explanation. I wanted the details of how he did it with her. I would not share and I would not let her have him. Of course, he agreed, but his eyes were sly and satisfied. Once I was finished with him, I set off to read her rights to that pint-sized slut.

I found her. She was fresh from a bath, half-dressed. A normal-sized man with delicate fingers attended her. I asked him to leave us. He smiled enigmatically and bowed. I took her from him and stepped aside to give him way. I sat her down on the edge of the huge sink of our bathroom.

"I came to tell you it's over," I said. "I will not share. If he disagrees, we'll divorce."

"I understand," she said, "And I quite agree."

She sat there, calm and serious, with her tiny legs crossed at the ankles. The explanations were over. I spoke a few more words then helped her to her feet. She froze.

"Well, go on then!" I said.

Her attendant appeared un-summoned, a present-day eunuch. There was really nothing new under the sun; men were still making toys, unmaking men, perverting love.

"Were you really speaking to *her*?" her attendant asked, incredulous. But I paid no attention to him. I had other matters to settle.

The Dance

"So who's praying for this bitch?" the man asked.

He stood there like a wrathful doorkeeper, his mouth rejecting the pips of sour grapes. Had he been a magnanimous murderer in a movie and I his prospective victim, he would have spoken to me directly, offering me time to say a last prayer. But he held no weapon and was not speaking to me.

His question was in French, to my friend Pierre. I didn't get it – I didn't know him, he'd been getting too close and I had stepped away. And we weren't in church, so maybe he meant 'paying'. Even then it didn't make sense. Was he using me to settle a score with Pierre? They probably knew each other. He had posed the question in French in a low rumble using the word *chienne*. His words stung. They riled me.

It's a bad thing to be a dog, human languages all agree. Love them as we might, our words of anger deny dogs any affection. A profound atavism, a forgotten memory decides that man's best friend is a vile beast. In these deep strata, gender places the female even lower than the male in the cloaca of lust and filth. The problem is that this stranger was talking about me, calling me a 'bitch'.

'Slut' would have been my mother's word– a reproach for whatever she saw as inappropriate behaviour in her daughters. Untidiness, nudity and late rising were all offensive to God and his angels. My mother, who kept watch, redressed us with the rod of a word: slut! That was long ago and far away, but now here was this man: because I didn't want him in my space, I was a bitch and needed prayers. Or some other sort of ransom.

His question pushed me out of sleep, out of bed.

Sitting up now, I drink the remains of yesterday's afternoon tea, English breakfast (well tea is tea) that I had shared with Pierre, now about to land on the other side of the Atlantic. Except for the slur from a strange man, I have lost all the threads of the dream. I cannot even recall the context of the man's question. But I understand its connection to a world where the need for redemption and the practice if not the efficacy of prayer are givens. Where my need for prayer is self-evident. Where the existence of a willing mediator seems dubious. I pull the remaining rough thread of the offensive stranger's words through my fingers, last night's anger behind me. But for some reason the question continues to trouble me.

Then I remember the dance.

Last night at Alfonso's party, an hour after I had been ready to leave, I danced a new dance, alone in the middle of an improvised dance floor, jamming with a djembe quartet. I invented a response to a musical motif I did not know. I danced until I could almost dance no more. Just short of that point, I stopped, denying myself other, new ways of responding to the call of the drums.

Afterwards – after the spectacle, not necessarily a good word – I explained to colleagues at the party who had admired – a word once tinged with horror in classic French – the way I'd let loose, that I had never, ever danced like that before. Despite twenty years in the Hausaland of Nigeria with its weekly afternoon wedding day dances. On Saturday's, before the rising tide of intolerance, women's richly clad rears had taunted overheated musicians. But as a classificatory aristocrat, that sort of dancing was out of bounds for me. As I am no dancer, I didn't mind. I would watch and clap and stick money on the sweaty faces of the dancers. Awkwardly, when pulled up from my seat, I would join in the more genteel dances with my sisters-in-law, our veils rhythmically waving. I never quite understood the rhythm of such dances. The slow shuffling bored me. I had never taken a serious one-woman stand in the middle of the dance circle, tackling the drums. I had seen Amina, a cousin-in-law dance a challenge to the drummers, kicking up the dust, working dexterous glutes till her wrapper slipped, exposing voluminous white panties to the circle of women, drummers, and a few extraneous gawkers. I had also observed the disgust of a senior aunt-in-law, Babani. She had said nothing, had simply pulled her veil of lace over the lower half of her thin face and had become totally rigid. I loved her particularly and would not have cared to be in Amina's shoes on that or any day. I never asked myself why Babani's approval was so important to me, but it was.

So last night's dance was a first for me – a troubling first, a stepping beyond the line. Another, if you count leaving Nigeria for good.

I was not alone in the idea that something exceptional had occurred. Our hostess, Lily's take was: "That was serious, Terry! You were exorcising demons!" Below a mass of square cut red curls, Lily's freckled face was serious. I was surprised. Exorcising demons? What demons?

Sometimes, it all boils down to words. Words thick with meaning, or words distilling meaning from observation and experience. Even seemingly harmless words like 'admire', as I recalled. Ad-mire'. To look (appreciatively) in the direction of someone or something is the common meaning in Latin-influenced languages. But in the French of three centuries ago, the word had had a stronger sense. Monsieur Joubert our eleventh grade French teacher had explained it memorably: the attracted gaze was also an astounded one. It was intense, filled with horror and other emotions. E-motions. There is action in that word, evoking feelings that agitate the body in their storm. Monsieur Joubert never got to find out, but his infectious passion for classic French theatre had impacted my life, weirdly contributing to my two decades-long relations with anti-twerking African aunts-in-law long before that dance craze hit North America.

At Alfonso and Lily's party, the gaze at my dance was not innocently appreciative. Take a word like "demons" coming from Lily, a sociolinguist with serious field practice of Africa. (Africa, here is merely Benin, but the monolith has a massive kick. Read the guidebook: Africa – its dances and demons. I too go for the kick, sometimes; in academia and in everyday life I indulge in the power of the generic.) Lily had seen me as battling with my demons.

I was disconcerted by the association with demons.

Even in their mildest connotations demons are not banal. To engage in a battle with a demon (or an angel) is to have a deep conversation with your soul. With your body. With another, invisible thing or host of things hiding inside you, sometimes manifesting, getting at you, riding you. Is that what it was about, my dance (since, the deed done, I must claim it)?

The aftershock of those long minutes was surprise (including my own), judgment (in the mildest sense, surely) and the conviction that something serious had happened. It was a protracted aftermath and continued with a nightmare in which a stranger insulted me. And this nightmare had had something to do with the dance of the night before, with what it meant. For surely it meant something?

I remember the dance now from its outer fringes. Gingerly. I keep it at arm's length with mind games. It – the dance in which I let loose, admirably – is still hot to the touch the morning after. It leaves me feverish with wonder. Was that *me*? I cannot return to the classificatory box that I had meekly entered after my marriage in Sokoto. I had walked away from that marriage. I have legally severed the ties, and am now free to make a new life for myself here in Central Florida. But apparently, I am not quite done with Nigeria.

Or it is not done with me. This is a morning after crisis. Coming out of my dream, out of my memory of the dance, I imagine that a deeply religious woman might have feelings similar to mine after a night of great sex with a stranger. Maybe a new love, but not one meant to go so fast, so far.

The man had said 'bitch' and 'pray'. My mother would have said 'slut'– a word thick with flesh and filth. The man had said 'pray'. Now, the morning after, with no trace of last night's orgy in my body, I keep thinking, 'pay'. It's still not clear. I regroup and return to last night.

〜〜〜〜

What really happened is this. Nadia, from Arabic Studies and I had enjoyed the drumming and would have loved to dance, but neither of us knew the rhythm.

"You go and I'll follow!" I urged Nadia.

She loves to dance and is good at it.

"No, *you* go and I'll follow!" Nadia demurred.

It was the same with Saada, from African Studies. This pretty young woman obviously enjoys dancing, but her native Senegal is far away. She had lived in France since age five. I didn't know the music. I had lived twenty years in Nigeria but I had 'belonged' to a social class whose women do not take centre-stage in the dance circle during wedding ceremonies, remember? And dancing had never come naturally to me. I had pursued it unsuccessfully for a good five years of dance training in Barbados and Switzerland. But years after I had abandoned the pursuit, it came all by itself, in its own way, in its own sweet time.

The dance that came thus is occasional party dancing or a short choreography during a gym routine; nothing savvy, just for fun. I'm still neither a dancer nor a party girl, but when the occasion arises, rarely, I have fun. But this was different. One minute I was pulling

Nadia's arm telling her to go first, the next minute I was all by my-self trying to follow what the drums were saying.

I had had a few glasses of wine and was too full to feel able to dance at all, in the beginning. But Nadia, Giulia from Linguistics and I had gone all crazy with our apron dance stunt, to show Alfonso that stacking the dishwasher was no trouble for us at all. Music was playing in the background. We stacked dishes to the music, singing and acting silly. Alfonso had made an elaborate and very tasty din-ner and had invited some really cool colleagues. An hour or so later, with the dishwasher whirring happily toward the end of the cycle and some order restored to the kitchen, I was ready to go home. I had said goodbye. Lily had asked me to stay a bit longer. The danc-ing was in full swing now. Wouldn't I stay for one more dance? No, really the party was awesome (I had started to use that empty word), but I was bushed, my first semester working at CFU had been chal-lenging. I was standing in the doorway, thanking Lily, when the drummers started setting up their instruments. She smiled entreaty, looking in their direction. Of course, I would stay and listen to their playing. A few minutes more would change nothing.

But soon we were playing together, the drummers and I – and 'my demons', if Lily was right.

How can I approach what happened in that small circle?

Afterwards, Pierre said he wished he had brought his camera so he could have filmed it for it was really *quelque chose*.

I inched up to what had happened in that small circle.

I had been in a private space, in public; tight within myself, my gaze turned in; not least because I dared not look out or engage with the attention of those around me. *At-tension.* The alertness, the silence around me, just beyond the drums.

I let the drums enter me, softly at first. I tried the floor with my feet. I tried the air with my arms. I flexed my knees from memory.

I let the drums open me up; I yielded to the back and forth of their rhythm; responded to the call. The music took me, led me, teased me, loosened me up then steered me onwards. It played with me. I played back. I improvised positions and propositions. I plotted the next move a second in advance. I let go. I relaxed. I exulted. I laughed and flexed into the beat. I called back. The call and response seemed unending. I forgot that I couldn't, that I shouldn't. I was tired, though. The drums slowed with me. Then I left the circle and collapsed into an armchair trying not to seem breathless.

"You look exhausted," Karen said.

I was exhausted. And troubled. Now what was that? It had felt good. But what was it?

~~~~

When Herek called, I was still wearing my favourite big tee-shirt, black with fluorescent pink graffiti down the front, urging me to *Live love play under the moonlight shine*. I was still deep in my morning-after anxiety. The phase where you know that you must be pregnant because it was the wrong time of the month and especially because it had been too good. And it had to be good for something beyond the pleasure.

My mind strays. Back to atavism: pleasure is not the point of sex. Just the bait. The point is procreation. Getting away with pleasure is illegal. Pleasure. Do the other animals experience it? Our dog in Zaria used to look sad and hooked and silly, waiting for the vagina of Halima's bitch to stop milking and release him. So what was his bait? Just getting high on someone else's steam: she smells hot and yummy; I want to get in on that? Why not eat her, then? But of course that's not how it works, the divinity that shakes our ends.

I was in a strange kind of morning after anxiety seeing that sex was not involved. What was I expecting?

I was alone with the thing that I had started. I was still spooked. I felt outlandish: an audacious bitch. A.B.: my new initials. A., in my own eyes; B., for some. I would live with it, with this new whatever.

Never mind the distractions, I was working through the dream and the dance when Herek called. Foolishly, I mentioned them. The dream. The dance. He said some trite crap about ass-shaking and regrets that showed he didn't get it; not at all.

Herek has the art of making my hackles rise, frequently, while remaining on my calling list. Ours is a quirky friendship. I just hate (and pity) his anti-Africa stances, for one (he is African, born and bred). Plus I don't take well to his teasing. But he is the only friend to whom I can say things in an uncooked language without giving offense. Tolerant with a sense of humour that you wouldn't suspect at times: that's Herek. Our conversations are my oases of free speech. But they are not perfect, and now Herek was being no help at all. I told him so, that he didn't understand. "Well, explain yourself!" he demanded (he always demands) in that snotty professorial way of his, his thick symmetrical lips curling back from huge teeth. I told him that I couldn't now, that I was working on it myself. I would let him know.

But I won't. It is my business, not his.

Nobody's paying for this woman. She's buying her own ticket for the dance.

Karim

"Had we met before?" he asked me the morning after, lying next to me, miraculously alive.

Karim is warm with lean hard muscles and baby-soft skin. I still have trouble putting these last two traits together and I can't stop touching him. I'm like someone who finally gets to indulge a craving, except that it's not like that at all. Not really, since I've only just met him, which is another miracle, as I can't see how life before him was even possible.

His face is like the first dawn. Fresh from the hands of his Maker, he is wondrously formed with just a hint of moisture and shining. We had met, of course, very recently and in a manner of speaking only; for when I set eyes on him for the first time, yesterday, he was newly dead, not yet cold and amazingly beautiful, still.

He had enjoyed his beauty, Samia told me, suddenly communicative in her grief, would I help to fix him up for burial, being a make-up artist and all? It was totally insane, but as she had never asked me for anything before, I accepted.

We had been friends, of sorts, for almost two years. For a year and a half, it had been fine. Samia isn't much of a conversationalist, but she has this nice face and something about her calmed me down and I liked that. I liked her voice saying something not important in that relaxing way of hers.

Our get-togethers went like this. Samia would call. Was I doing something special tonight? It was always short notice. I am, well was, never doing anything special at night. I need a lot of time to unwind. Before Karim, that is. Well, before yesterday, really. I touch the miracle of Karim's butt and it stays there, hard as iron, soft as satin and it's all dreamy and wonderful. I wish I could just let it go and not probe it, but I find that I can't erase Samia. Not completely. So she'd call and I would go over and we'd be there, at her place until late, drinking cup after cup of tea and eating the spicy food she said was not spicy because of me. And I'd be there, my mouth on fire, drinking tea to cool the heat, but cosy as anything all the same. It was nice at Samia's, with all those cushions and colours and textures from her country, and I would have trouble tearing myself off her couch, away from her voice, to go home and sleep.

Then Karim came along and things changed. She rarely spoke about him and I never met him at her apartment. In fact, she stopped inviting me over, and I never met him at all. I knew that they had met, that she was madly in love and different, suddenly loquacious on all subjects but one, and too busy of course, which I could understand. I missed her and resented her, but life went on.

It went on for nearly six months, then once again there she was calling me on the phone, urgently; talking about Karim and his death and his beauty and about needing me to see to him for the last time as if I'd had ever seen him before. I closed my salon, it was close to closing time anyway, took my entire cosmetic kit, not knowing what colours I would need, and went to join her at the mortuary.

He had loved himself, she said, simply; no bashfulness or false pride. No hypocrisy. Tears made Samia's large brown eyes brighter than ever; tears that were against the rules, so she told me, unable to help herself. Tears ran down the pure lines of her face, making her alive in a manner I had never witnessed before. That aliveness had been part of their hidden story and now there it was, out in the open, but what was the point?

I couldn't see his eyes. What was his name, again? Yes, Karim. I couldn't see Karim's eyes, but from what I could see they must have formed a beautiful pair, he and Samia; beautiful and invisible. And now I was seeing them together for the first time in the preparation room of a mortuary. It made no sense at all. What did this have to do with me? Why now? He had lived, beyond my knowledge, why involve me now that it was over? Something hard awoke in me, but there I was. Afterwards, I would have to replace all the brushes and cosmetics I was about to use on his body.

Had he died in an accident? If so, it had not spoiled him. But that was temporary. He had to be put away very soon before he became the opposite of what he had always been. And because he had been a Muslim until a few short hours ago, the sooner he was put away was deemed the better, for the good of his soul.

Even here in exile, rules had to be respected, even in the life of those two who had lived independent of the rules, private and happy for six months. Almost. But now that his days were done, the home country was alive again, to Samia. If it could, if it knew, it would have stretched its tentacles across the Atlantic to guide and regulate. But now its arms were short of a length, or retracted in vengeance. In the lonely North, they were on their own; the two of them. They had wanted this. Had wanted to have nothing come in between them, had suffered only inevitable separations: the dictates of earning a living and the envelopes of Samia's dark brown pelt and Karim's golden hide. These last thin barriers they had crossed night after night aided by their appendages, large and small. There had been no space for family and friends. So, that now there was no one left to call on, I had come to Samia's mind; now that she was all alone.

Karim had been a world in himself. He had brought bounty to the table. Death had not been on the agenda. But is it ever when you are happy, young and beautiful?

Call Catherine, she had thought. Call Catherine now, she will understand. She will come. Karim would not be inhumed according to the rites of the old country. That was out. A last viewing was in order. And he must be prepared, must shine one last time in facial splendour, a caftan covering all the rest up to the chin.

The mourners would come after work. They would not ask questions. It was the custom at home, to dispose of the body quickly. There would be no problem with the law. A certificate had been delivered, and the body released. She had decided to cremate him.

The woman at the mortuary had stared at the immediacy, but, yes it could be done, since it was not a burial. The mourners would not like it, but what could they do? Karim had only her, and now that he was gone, it was for her that they would come, knowing that this country is crazy. Her words tumbled out, barely coherent.

So, we were to be friends again? I wondered about this but did not refuse. I did not refuse although my work had always been for the living.

Karim.

So there he was, at last, a young god asleep. His face was a study in gold and brown and bronze with the faintest hint of fading pink. Instinctively, I wanted Samia to leave so I could work in peace, but that was impossible, so I steeled myself and got going.

How can I express what happened next?

How I raised him slightly for a picture with her, my hands under his armpits, and how he awoke, the whites of his eyes white like milk. A man. A god. A thing of earth and sky. A masterpiece.

And then we were alone. He was naked up to the waist, still in his winding sheet, and I was nude and long and dark, stretched across his legs, held in his arms. I had come home.

"But how was it going to be, with Samia and all?" My eyes questioned him.

"My time has not yet come," he said.

Of course, I understood. He meant about the social things. Facing people. Explaining. But it would come. It would come, surely. Very soon.

Granpa Joseph

B ack then, at the beginning of the twentieth century, it was unusual for a man to take a wife or paramour with him on his adventures in Cuba, Colon, that they also call Panama, you know, Costa Rica, Ecuador, Nassau; anywhere you could find work. It was unusual, but it happened. And sometime one or two own-way woman found the way right over there to challenge you, and sometime you love a woman till you fool, and the life's too hard alone, and you know she is a stalwart, a warrior, so you send for her, to battle together.

But it is a risky thing to do, very risky; and a man rarely tried it. Adventure, as the name says, is a precarious thing, you know, not steady, not steady at all. Taking a wife or a sweetheart means settling. And in this life abroad, in Cuba and Central America, Nassau and some other places like Venezuela, Colombia that you run to when the hard life hit you (it was mostly the Spanish places in those days that had work, plenty work) things were rough, very rough, dark sometimes, you couldn't see your way. You had to move, move, move fast, run here, stop there, scuffle, hustle, batter 'bout, live bad. You had the strangeness, the language that you don't know when you first arrive, it's just sign language, talking with your hands and screwing up your face, feeling like a jackass, till you pick up the lingo. You had the cold, and the *poto-poto*, your feet in water and mud all the time, in some places. And is cut cane till you back bruck, carry and load till you weak, walk, walk, run, drive cart if you lucky and you smart or if you have a good trade, one that they need. Always on the run, at harvest time. Not to say anything about cut-up hand and insect-bite and blister-foot, for there is much worse, like the bad fever they have over there plenty in Cuba, kill off many a strapping, strong man, or send him home mash-up, broke. When the crop finish, now, and everything dead down, life is slow, slow, dull. You have to use your brains, find something to get money to send home, to the parents, to the Missis and the pickney-dem. It was no joke, you know, no joke.

It is funny, you know; Cuba or Ecuador or Jamaica, in a way, it was the same thing; and then again it was not the same thing. One place or another it was hard labour. In Jamaica: working the land, burning coal, chipping logwood, or working a trade, like carpenter or cabinet maker, tailor, shoemaker and such the like. Mostly, even for a tradesman, same thing for the seamstress, and even the little profession-dem like teacher, postman, policeman, and pastor for those who went further in school, you couldn't do just one thing to make a living, no sir! The pay was a misery. A pittance. Almost everyone had to farm ground, whether you black or you brown, you have to secure the food, and money was scarce in Jamaica, almost as scarce as fowl teeth.

So it was a life on the move, you see, from a long time back, from slavery time. Same thing when slavery was done. It was pure moving but not the same kind, you know, not the same kind. Some moving was not of your making, people come, big arms, gun and cannon with plenty fire, big ship that you never see before, them come, them catch you, them move you, tie you up in a dark stinking hole, with plenty wailing and rolling 'bout in the sea, just rocking and shaking, vomiting, diarrhoea and disease, real hell. There, if you get a chance, you can make a move: jump overboard when they bring up to douse you with cold seawater, to make sport making you dance to secure that the stock, that is you and those like you, bound done below in the evil pit, don't perish all before arrival. Or you can kill a man and let them kill you in return. Or you can stay down there and kill your spirit until your body perish as well. Or, if you know how to do it, you can stifle yourself by swallowing your tongue. Or you can consider how to work out some salvation in case this rolling devil-machine land somewhere one day. If you do any of these things, or something that comes from *you*, that is your move.

Then there is the moving that you decide for yourself if and when you reach, and you do it. You might say, "no!" and run 'way. That is your own moving during slavery time. Some time they catch you again, bring you back, chain you up, hand and foot, chain with spike round your neck, put you in the bilboes, whip you, make other man shit in your mouth. If you manage it, you kill a man or you run off again. That is your choice, your move. Sometimes, some places, you can't run go nowhere, the land flat, them have toll gate and watchman you have to get a pass to go anywhere, so you work your brains. When you're bound, you must obey.

That was slavery time; you still have to find your food, you still have your wife and pickney-dem to feed. You work till you drop down and the little food that them give you, little bit a sal' thing like shad or herring, mackerel, saltfish, salt beef, a few plantains and a little flour and corn meal, peas and so on, when you do get anything, can't keep a soul alive. You still have to cultivate the little piece of land that they allot you. And it is not charity, you know, for is them same one, the white backramassa-dem, drinking your sweat. Then, it is need that moves you: a man must live, a man must try to be a man and feed him pickney-dem.

It was the same way for the women folk, same way. Now, in that situation, if you drape up your old patched trousers, draw the waist-string tight, girth up your loins, and decide to push harder to work to find food to eat and left over to sell and make a little money; that move is your move. When you can, you know, when you can, and is not always that you can, but if you see an opening and you force the dead-weight fatigue out the way, and do a little business, right there, in miserable slavery, that is your move. This is the kind of move that make a man rise up, tall, proud, strong, despite everything. True, true; that is what the old-time people that remember tell my sister, Erna, and she tell me.

Now, even after we fight for freedom, and fight and fight, and them come with paper that say is freedom time, Jubilee, the hard life is the same way. Plenty hard work, almost no money, little or no land. You try to buy, you try to rent. Sometimes, you inherit, because even in slavery time some people use the money that they scuffle to buy their freedom and some land! Land, it is very important you know, very important. Those who have no land or who have a little land that is not fertile or too dry, the struggle that they struggle can't finish, can't finish, at all, at all, neither for them nor for their generation. So, if you have no land, or no good revenue from land, trade can't help you much for there is no money to pay you most of the time, no matter how good your work is, and you decide to move to a better parish, where the land is fatter, like Clarendon, Portland and so, then that move is also your move.

There was a lot of tramping up and down the land in search of a living, in a quest for betterment; St Elizabeth to Clarendon, Clarendon to Bog Walk, Bog Walk to Kingston, all over the place. You would think Jamaica was a continent, not a little island, for there was not much transportation, or any you could easily afford, is just walk upon foot, train eleven, you two feet, one before the other, you trot like a donkey, over the land, anywhere you have to go, unless it is a far way, like to Kingston. That was the case for most people; they couldn't afford no mount, horse or mule or donkey, much less a dray cart, for where was the money? To possess those things, you needed to be a person of substance!

Many move to Kingston after trying the other parishes. Some that have no land and heart-sick of the plantation and the white people pushing them around, despite the Jubilee talk, pressuring and taxing them to prevent them trying to fend for themselves outside the wickedness of the cane-field; they move to Kingston direct or indirect, first chance they find.

It is the landless peasant that turned into townie the quickest. But Kingston too was hard, no matter all the pretty story they used to tell 'bout tram car and gas lamp and tall brick building, and nice frame house, big stores with all the things that come from England and all over. Kingston was hard, unless you have a good trade and some luck too. And St. William Grant Park and Missis Queen 'pon her white-foot stone horse couldn't change that, for is not your father own Myrtle Bank Hotel, and your mother might get a job to clean room in there if she's lucky, and can swallow her pride, or she can sell boobey-egg in front of it if she is not, or if she can't stand the servant work. Anyway, as a countryman in town, without land, catching hell, you pray for the day when someone will come in from your mountain with a big basket of food, a couple bunches of banana and some corn pork to give you, to help you out.

But some find work in factory, on the wharf, in the Jubilee Market, and all those places, and they improve themselves. Send their children to school and when they finish, to trade. But the living wasn't easy, no space, same one-room, one room-and-hall, if you're lucky, and no ground to plant a little food, remember! Others come and go, from country to town, selling provisions, coal or grass and so on. Others stay, doing domestic work, man and women, do it; another slavery that hide its name. Not nice, at all.

But Kingston has one big doorway that opens wide for a man to make his move, that is Kingston Harbour. Many a man came and went through that door for decades. For some, it was *the door of no return*; Kingston Harbour to Santiago then silence, blackout. Not another word out of some of these men that migrate. Sick catch them. Death catch them. Life move them far, over sea, over land; they leave from Cuba, sail to Panama, track overland to somewhere else. Some can't settle, they move and move till the Saviour call them home; sometimes, very early; before the time. Others just settle down same place, where life disembarks them, with a woman from there, and the new life is a force turning their head always in front, always in front, no looking back. Back there, Jamaica is too far, too long. *The earth is the Lord's and the fullness thereof, the world and they that dwell therein.* It is just life, a thing too big for a man to take up and put on his head. Life is not a hampa basket, you know. Sometimes if you try to hoist it on your head it just bruck your neck. No skylarking, this is the God-truth. So, they just grow where they planted. That is life for you; it is not simple, and then again it can be simple, it all depends on your outlook. But even back then, my outlook was progressive.

Back then, at the beginning of the twentieth century, it was unusual for a man to take a wife or paramour with him on his adventures in Cuba, Colon, that they also call Panama, you know, Costa Rica, Ecuador, Nassau, all dem places. But I was a progressive man, and I took Annie-May with me. Married her wid a ring 'pon her finger and took her and the two children with me to Ecuador. One piece a struggle. And you know that one day she get a telegramme telling her that her Modder dead, and I scuffle up everything for her passage wid the children, so she put her Modder away decent, and a neva see her again?

Woman to Woman

I ignore precisely what demons of anger and resentment my mother raised or exorcised when she recited the Psalms of David? What I know is that something snapped inside her after the eighteen months of grief during which she lost her first son, her only surviving brother, and her aged mother; something that lighting candles and praying to the Virgin assuaged but could not mend.

My mother was not raised as a Catholic. The liturgy of the Church did not match her soul, but for years she had tried it, until she eventually found her way into a Pentecostal church. That was in the early 90s, when I was far away, in another world.

From this world, I can see my mother, but she cannot see me. She does not love this unknown world that has swallowed me. Nevertheless, I take her there on the wings of story.

I raise my mother now in a candle-lit séance to learn what demons retreated while she kneeled intoning alien Catholic prayers. I revive her images.

This one, the feat of carrying-water-in-a-basket that poor people must perform, is no secret to me. I too performed it, and I have not forgotten. She was never sure that I had perfected that ever-changing skill. She did not know how long I would need it.

She did not know that she was my light and that I would always be able to go back to her. I did not know this, either.

～～～

To lift the weight of body and mind, my mother lights a cheap candle and invokes a strange woman with an improbable destiny, Mary the Mother of Christ. On her knees, my mother rises up against her lot in life.

"Man dat don like you, give you basket feh carry wata."

But nothing is impossible for those who are smart.

"You take mud patch it."

The mud my mother used to make a basket hold water was not just prayer. But she prayed a lot. She prayed and she struggled, and prayed some more.

"Oly Mary, modder of God, pray for us sinners now and at de our of our deat. Amen."

Again and again and again; in sheaves of ten, Hail Marys tumble over her bosom. Her tired knees are bent before Mammy, her mother's old dressing table, on which stands a fast-melting candle. Higher up, on an old cabinet with most of its treasures broken, the slightly stronger glow of a kerosene lamp, with its home-sweet-home shade and worn almost groove-less neck, slowly succumbs to a gathering of soot. Even higher, the ceiling-less roof with its blackened zinc sheets and visible beams crackles above her head. Releasing the stored heat of the day, the roof now crackles and pops. When it is not seared by sun, it is chastised by rain, which leaks through in places, with a plop-plop-plop into basins and pails.

"Pray for us, sinners; now and at the hour of our deat. For we know not the hour. He will come like a thief in the night. He will come and be welcome, takin de burden down. Down. Down."

My mother's litany drones deep into the night while neighbourhood thieves and rapists breach flimsy doors. They swing M16s and AK47s like Hollywood gangsters on TV. Last month, on Balactra Rd, Vie-vie was raped before her children. After that Cheryl, Vie-Vie's older daughter, hated herself. Thinking that the man with gun was coming for her, after finishing with her mother, she had pointed out her sister, Kay to the rapist.

"Take har, she bigga dan me," Cheryl had bargained, terrified.

But afterwards, Cheryl despised herself, not the criminal. Two nights later, she doused her pink nylon nightie with kerosene oil, donned it, and struck a match. She sparked like a flame in the night, before her charred body was taken to the Kingston Public Hospital. There it agonized for days, naked under netting.

On Worthly Avenue, Miss Hopeland's brains spattered the dead body of her son, Delroy. The old woman had refused to release her crazed clutch of protection on her last boy, when the boys from Seaview came to get him.

"Pray for us sinners now, for poverty is a crime and we are guilty; from generation to generation; left and right: the politicians, the gunman dem: the United States, Cuba, Russia, and Jamaica. The fathers eat the sour grapes, the chilrens' teet on edge."

<hr />

In the folk way, my mother's prayer waxes epic and biblical in the midst of the night, no matter that she has never heard the word 'epic' in her life. All she knows is work, and watch, and wait. When sleep evades her, she prays: when life preys on her, she prays.

"Pray for us sinners now. Souls are falling. Have mercy on the fishermen in the night sea. Leviathan roves the deep and the Most High sees him.

Behold, the young lions cry to Him and are fed. The cattle on a thousand hills are His.

His, the earth and the fullness thereof, the world and they that dwell therein.

His, the young lions to be fed. His, too, the gentle deer that bounds no more. His, the lion's jaws.

For God is good and shall not allow your feet to falter. Lest my enemy say he has prevailed against me, and those who hate me rejoice when I am moved.

No rest for the wicked. Tonight, tonight again, Lord, if I live, I live; if I dead, I dead."

～～～

On nearby Antigua Rd., an M16 blasts off in the night. People get flat; they lie low or scramble for cover.

"Dem bust shot! Is who dead now? Is who dead?"

In my own night, I seek my mother's praying form. She is dozing on her knees. Is she tired of fleeing the present, of coaxing the future?

But the cramps in her stiff limbs revive her. She creaks upright. Holding the edge of a worn mattress, she displaces the outermost body of a sleeping child and stretches out on her left side, facing the closed louvers that let in the orange glare of the streetlight. But sleep eludes her still, for hours, until the goo of morning oozes out from the eye corners of the night.

～～～

I return to those and other better nights and from their mornings after. I search them, tempted to mock myself: what light can you find in darkness? But I cannot mock. This is not a game. I look. I do not close my eyes.

One night they kill Chineeman Willie, who owns the corner shop; another night, they mow down Lascelles; one night, it is the turn of Mr. Lyons … One night, one night, one more night in the life of nasty neyga.

Bust shot! Get flat!

Popular reggae artists make a song out of the vocabulary of inner city violence. Weekend revellers have fun getting flat. The scramble for survival becomes the new dance craze. One night, a popular politician, D.K.D., at a political party rally in the neighbourhood, in front of dead Willie's shop, strikes the gangster pose, gun in hand, to show the ruling party's will to put an end to criminals from the opposition.

The nation is divided between those who bust shot and those who get flat. The government mandates the police to shoot first, and ask questions later. The police too join the ranks of 'bust shot, get flat'. They kill and are killed, while journalists keep the score from hearsay.

The commotion of gunfire is not the only enemy of my mother's sleep. Inside her, too, sorrows gnaw at tight nerves. When sleep comes, finally, it is almost time to rise with sour breath and aching bones and trod on.

Another day.

What are the dreams that visit my mother's short, restless sleep, night after night, while the floodlights of army helicopters remind the delinquent poor that the government is watching, that crime does not pay?

Does she dream of a life where you can eat all the hard dough bread and salted butter you want after a day's sweat in the tropical heat? Does she see a new heaven and a new earth? And what if they don't exist? What if it's only a fairytale? What if it's real, but only in this life, and only for the fortunate? If so, she must pray that we, her children, will be fortunate. To help ourselves, but to help, her too, of course.

Naturally.

But for me, it never worked out. She died before I could help her. I was in a land far, far away, where no milk and honey was flowing; where there had been a uranium boom, but now there was a slump.

She died, unaided by me, but I will not let her rest because I need her.

Still.

Dreading to dream, my mother succumbs to hopeful visions so that she may live and not die. My mother does not rest. Rest requires peace and my mother can have no peace. Poverty is a sin, a sin.

Confession brings no absolution; not with this sin, no. The sins of the fathers will visit the children until the third and fourth generation. So says the good book.

In a world beyond my mother's, unknown to her, other people say savvier things, that change nothing. Social reproduction. Structurally entrenched evil. Mismanagement. The last powdering of the Cold War. Miserabilism. Congenital sloth.

"You people are just lazy! No damn ambition! All you do is drink, and fuck, and breed like rabbits!"

The poor are evil. Whether they sleep or work, they catch hell.

~~~

My mother walks in the hot sun from Pembroke Hall to Waterhouse across Washington Boulevard, across Coore Bridge, across the gully where dead bodies turn up bagged and tagged, with a box of frozen chicken necks and backs on her head. She sells them on the late Chineeman Willie's piazza to pay her children's schooling.

At night, she prays, lying on her back, kneeling on her knees. By day, she sighs out ejaculations, as Catholics call short invocations of the Most High:

"Saviour Divine!"

"Lord, have mercy! Christ, have mercy! Angels, have mercy! Have mercy! Have, Mercy!"

"Saviour at the cross I stand!"

~~~

Does she dream of a land flowing with milk and honey? Does anyone? Does my mother dream?

One night, asleep once again on her knees, my mother has a vision of a woman her age, with superior laughing eyes. A woman who walks in beauty and power, who says that the real beauty, the real power is inside; a woman she does not know, but who knows her, knows her name.

The woman mocks her gently.

"Queenie, my dear, you have not lived; only two men in your life? No, one; for the first was a boy and you did not get the chance to know him. Does the hanger-on, who has waited for hours, cracking jokes, sniffing the aroma of the stew pot, know the taste of the food when he is not invited to stay for dinner?"

What foolishness is this? Who is this woman? Her oval face is framed in a veil of transparent white cotton edged with lace. She comes from a land far away, a land that is foreign and not foreign, with black people like herself, unlike herself. You can tell. But why has she come? Why does she smile so, her black eyes brilliant, her braids shining with oil?

The woman maintains that she, my mother, has not lived, has not lived by half, may speak only of children, but not of men or love; for what does she know?

This liberty-taking woman in her vision has something to do with her lost daughter, but what precisely? In a flash, she guesses the connection, but her insight quickly vanishes; it mounts up into a cone of ultra-fine sand, then dissipates as quickly as it came. Before the ever-narrowing funnel of sand disappears, the veiled woman bows to it. My mother, too, inclines her grey head. When she looks up, she has lost the connection between the woman and her lost daughter, between the woman and herself. But it does not matter. The woman, lightly veiled, is still standing before her.

The woman says they are the same age. She says her that her name is Rockyah, or something like that. She claims that she, Rockyah, has lived so much that she is tired of living, tired of men.

"Nine children and nine husbands! All nine children with the first husband. Nine children, one by one, no twins, no miscarriages, no stillbirths; all with the first man, do you hear?"

A great task accomplished, done in ninety moons! After that she, Rockyah by her own will and through her own knowledge, had closed her womb. She was done with bearing children and done with her first husband, too.

"Sixteen years is a long time, time enough to know your right foot from your left, your head from your ass!"

After sixteen years, the marriage had lost its flavour, like the trash of *areke,* of sugarcane held too long in the mouth. She spat it out. She had lost the taste for *that* marriage, or rather, it had lost its taste; there was no sweetness there.

"Tell me, my dear, what is the use of spending sixteen more years finding out whose fault…?"

She married again. She had lost the taste for a particular man, but not for love. Her second husband was sweet, a sweeter man you could not find. But after a few years he was no longer sweet. She left him. People gossiped; people always gossip: *baki abun magana,* mouth is made for chat; let it do its work, for good, for evil. Men made remarks. They spoke about her to one another. They went home with a swell in their loins, a gleam in their eyes and water in their mouths. At night, after the Maghrib prayer, they came, damp from their ablutions. They courted. They begged, praising her beauty, ignoring the words of their mothers and womenfolk. She chose another, then another. A third marriage, then a fourth, a fifth. Sugarcane chewed too long becomes hay in the mouth and she is not a horse.

"The fifth man was a wonder, but he died."

Wonders ever cease. She mourned him for a full year, beyond the demands of custom. Then she became lonely in the cool months of the harmattan and started to develop bad thoughts. Another man came to console her. He was heavy-set and serious, but divinely elastic in the hips, with a way of shuddering in the moment of delight. The final waves of his pleasure were tantalizingly communicable. They were man and wife for three years. He wanted children, but she was done with child bearing; she had nine children; and he had two by a woman who had gone back to her father's house, far away. She released him. They remained friends. She married a sixth, then a seventh then an eight husband.

"Time goes by so quickly! The hardest part of a journey is the first step. After a short while, you marvel at how far you have gone. So it is my sister, so it is. God's truth! The road of life is long and not long: a day of love lasts a thousand years, and a day of love lasts less than a day; and pain never ends till it's over, and after pleasure there is more pleasure."

The seventh husband took her to Abidjan. There he worked long days, played cards till late, drank *chapalo*. Then, he became a devotee of the *hauka* and spent all day Sunday worshipping his deities of fire on the outskirts of town.

Had she not had her fill of religious types, like her second and fourth husbands who prayed to Allah all night, murmuring the sacred *suras* of the Koran, beyond knowledge, beyond sleep, in quest of the visions and prophecies ordered by their clients (the millet of life earned through spiritual sweat)?

The second husband wanted to ride her at noon, after she had worked all morning and the sun was high, a bad time for copulation if ever there was one. She left her seventh husband to his work on the docks of Abidjan by day, to his cards by night, and to his trances on Sundays and returned to Madaoua.

Her eighth husband – blessings upon him! – took her to Mecca, the doorway to paradise. But soon paradise was no longer in the bedroom at night. She prepared herself with special herbs, sat over burnt perfumes to fumigate her femininity, pounded spices for his food – spices that make men bold and free, she consulted the *boka*. His previous wife was working with the spirits to break their marriage. She let her have him.

"For, tell me dear, what is the point of running after one man, or hanging on to another? Is the world not full of men, from Madaoua to Mecca?"

She married again, for the last time. One hot day in April, the man started an argument about the price of provisions. She told him that a beautiful woman does not stay beautiful by eating *gari* and oil alone; *gari*, a food first brought to Niger in a memorable year of famine, the *garijiire*, the Zarmas name it, and oil not even fit to be rubbed into the soles of one's feet! Had he looked at her before talking such foolishness in the heat of the day?

He too wanted children. He insinuated that she was eating only to nourish the *salanga*, the pit latrine, and ploughed her body furiously in his obsession to plant children there, although he already had ten from three previous marriages.

"The fool! Did he think that making children was like planting yams? Didn't he know that wise women have always known how to make children and how to prevent them, since the world was young? And had they not negotiated their conditions at the beginning?"

While she varied not one iota in her bargain, he had forgotten, counting perhaps on the fabled inconstancy of woman. Well, she would not be ploughed by night and nagged by day in the middle of May, the worst month of the year. A man who cannot feed his wife and keep his word is no man. Besides she was fifty-eight and no longer interested. She had married for the first time at eighteen, a man of her choice.

"Forty years well filled and no regrets. Time to move on!"

She understood this when her only fantasies were those of her dead fifth husband, a wonder of a man. Men continued to come and plead at night. Some went down on their knees. She left Madaoua and went to Niamey to live at her brother's house. She joined his wife in learning the Koran at *makaranta*, and rested her case.

Now the recitation of *suras* of the Koran light her way at night.

"There is a time for every purpose under the heavens," says Rockyah, adding as an afterthought "But you *do* know about the love of children, my sister, more, in fact than I do. I left mine each time I married. But then, there is a time for everything, a time for passion, a time for peace; to each her own way in this life. As long as we make peace with ourselves, before the end of the day…"

So says Rockyah, before gathering up her veil and fading into the night.

Does she say all this for my mother or for me?

The Trip Back Home

For Andrea Francis

'm fifty-five years old, but today I feel ninety and heavy. I should be high right now, or maybe just loose and relaxed as our Delta Airline flight lifts over the green mass of Santo Domingo and angles towards Miami. I should be feeling as sprucey as Diego looks, his handsome young face bent over pictures of the twins on his iPad. I can feel the warmth of Diego's thigh, can almost sense his breath, but although he is (or was) my buddy, my colleague, my saviour, I cannot share Diego's contentment.

His twin – Alisha is the name she goes by – is looking up into Diego's face as if he were a god. Her skin looks orangey on the screen, but I know what it is like, how lovely it must be, in the sun, on the beach, against the white of fresh sheets, against the brown of Diego's perfect chest.

My twin, Shawna – her trade name – is not on this shot, just her arm around my neck. It is not a good shot. I look flabby and decrepit. My belly pulled in tight, not candid, my butt splayed uncontrollably over the white cushions of a bamboo chaise lounge at Coco Beach Club. Coco Beach Club! Talk about imagination! I've had too much to drink and my mouth in the picture is red and slack. Though Shawna, outside the frame, smiles and fawns on me, we both know that with us it is a hundred per cent professional.

His twin is professional, too, but there is no doubt that she feels Diego's heat, that she's having a good time and dreaming hard of a life with him in America. Of course, Diego is single. And Shawna would have accepted immediately had I been free to offer her the dream life in Florida. (How perfect and flowery that state must have sounded to her in her mother tongue, in her native deprivation, were it not for the Coco Beaches of her half of the island.) But we would both have known what was in the bargain had it been otherwise and I would not have hoped. Alisha had no reason to hope either.

This holiday, which took me three months to accept, was about us getting a great suite with communicating bedrooms and fucking a couple of bitches at the week-end after our conference. Diego's words. With no malice intended. Pure, beyond deceit. Generous even: we were going to go at those bitches without letting them come between us, so no closed doors. This was to be my therapy. I had been too damn *lofty* and depressed of late. The bitches would be gorgeous and ready, well treated, thus happy. A win-win situation.

I am a thinking man, it's my profession, and I understand these things. Diego and I are colleagues in the Department of International Business Communication at Y.C.U., so I know why Diego is doing everything except talking and joking with me as we usually do, easily, like good buddies the world over, slapping my shoulder and calling me *Davie, man*. I don't want to get lofty about this, but I can't help feeling that I have unwittingly engaged a battle with an angel and lost. Although Diego has been, up to a day ago, my saviour in a very real sense, he is not at home with the things he dismisses as *lofty* or *crap*. He didn't have to be. He was the thing itself, the redeemer embodied, who had no need to say his own name to himself over and over again in the mirror.

I turn away from Diego's face (his gently receding hairline, his sharp nose gone from gold to brown, the soft curl of his lips, the shadow of his holiday beard, the sweetness of his breath that I always noticed when he would bend to say something to me, real low). I look out the window. Below, the Caribbean is a postcard of blue sea, white sand and green mountains, inviting nostalgia.

Irrelevantly, I wonder about the etymology of the 'nost' in nostalgia. The 'algia' part is easy, of course; as easy as Diego's hand on a woman's ass when he is dancing, a groovy, grinding angel partial to flesh, even at a price.

The flight attendant serves fruit juice. I choose mango. For some reason it makes me think of Margaret, who is nothing like a mango. Still, when I was dating her, wilfully working to get her guard down, I had written a poem about that battle. It turned up the day after I accepted the principle of Diego's post-conference therapy and I'd slipped it into the side pocket of my computer bag. I had titled the poem "Mango", had entrusted to paper my strange, ungenerous intentions regarding Margaret's angular body:

Massage you till you're nice and soft
Mango flesh
Juice in the skin
Thick around the seed
Sweet
Between my tongue and teeth
On my lips
Liquid food sublime
Supine in my strong fist.

My intention was predatory, my youth candid, the ethos of my metaphor Jamaican. Macho. My father is Jamaican. He had come from Jamaica, had met and impregnated my mother while picking oranges as a farmworker in Florida in the late 50s, then had gone back home to his mountains, leaving us behind in the swamps.

Before flying to Kenya in 1985, I had gone to Jamaica in search of him and had also met my grandmother, Dolorita Mercedes Malcolm, who was still alive and active, quite toothless, and full of pithy mirth. Her technique for devouring a Bombay mango fascinated me. She'd hold the fruit in her strong fist and massage it gently, concentration on her brow, her lips sucked in in anticipation. When the priming was over, her nubby fingers would pinch out a funnel from the tip of the fruit and she would proceed to suck out the pulpy juice. Last would come the extraction and licking of the seed. I remembered her when courting Margaret. Afterwards, I would go home to my junior lecturer's studio at the University of Nairobi. The night would still be young as the young lady's parents had principles, and I would slouch in a too low itchy armchair, one hand cradling my crotch, the other a bottle of cold beer, and think of an old woman on a mountain sucking a mango.

Margaret had two exquisite features: a pretty mouth and lovely feet. It was at these extremities that I humbled myself when she came by, on Saturdays only, to bring me dinner. To see us relating now, with the boys grown and gone, leaving the house empty, full of pride and guilt and nostalgia for their young energy, you couldn't imagine me touching her at all. Well, you couldn't if you could really see us, which of course you can't as we're perfect in public by tacit accord. In our public truce we forget the separate beds, the separate cooking, the separate lives and talk about each other fondly. David just lo-oves a party, well… when he gets the time! Margaret is so organized; she always stays on top of it!

One December evening in 1985 in Nairobi, with dinner devoured and praised, I let myself be drawn deeper than usual into Margaret's mouth, following the opening and closing of her pouty lips, the glint of light on her perfect teeth, the full exposure of her pink tongue as she laughed gustily, her only release concentrated in that laughter. At that moment, I was easily persuaded that I loved her. The fact, though, was that as an African American expatriate in the motherland I was lonely and Margaret, a professor's daughter, didn't take me too far offshore. That was where the familiarity stopped. She was a formidable hinterland in other respects and her family, nice people really, were also and most importantly bastions of protestant bourgeois respectability. From feudality into modernity, they had held their rank. It had to be serious or nothing. I was thirty-five and longing for roots and family and Margaret was quite suitable though not precisely my type: too proper, too tight. I set about loosening her up.

I remember the first time I cradled Margaret's cold left foot in the palm of my right hand the way many remember their first kiss. I was kneeling before her, head bent, so she could not see my emotion, huge against my thigh, invisible inside my stomach, beating against my ribs, burning my palm. She looked down at me curiously, like a child watching some small, harmless creature, sure that David wouldn't… David's grandfather was a pastor. David sometimes goes to church with us. David is a brilliant young colleague of my dad's. David is, you know, soo sweet. Right now, there was nothing that David wouldn't do for the owner of a foot as delectable as Dolorita's mango. So, humble at her feet, I courted Margaret.

The rest is history and best left in memory's shroud, all except that twilight, when after weeks of upwardly mobile strategic foot massages, Margaret gave up her juice, arced in a cry that had nothing to do with her frame or genealogy.

I held her thin body in my arms. She clasped me within the fleshy sweetness of her vulva. I wept. Margaret was fat inside, fleshy in her secret way. She conceived. I married her, of course, disinclined to worsen the relations between Africa and the Diaspora. David is such a gentleman. East African lilting over the *gentle* in gentleman, elevating me from my humble, un-narrated, inenarrable beginnings, lost somewhere between the fragrance of Florida oranges and the stench of Florida swamps.

Two robust, splendid boys were born to us out of Margaret's improbable frame. Baby giants. Young gods. My wife's nipples, like two large raisins when she was aroused, were not equal to the task of breast-feeding. Our first son, Jason, made them bleed and was quietly transferred to the less susceptible nipples of a bottle. Our second, John, got just what was needed to bolster his immunity from his self-sacrificing mother.

Within five years, Kenya had revealed its limits career-wise, and Margaret's character had fallen into place. For one thing, the ritual journey from her feet up to the middle passage was banned; no more mangoes on the mountaintop. My wife had little sympathy for orally fixated males, regardless of age. For career reasons, my return home became inevitable. I also nourished the hope that America would broaden my wife's views.

It expanded her activities: activism in church and politics, a PhD, a penchant for sports and organization, a reputation as a charismatic, caring professor, a new mode of mothering; but the middle passage remained perpetually out of oral bounds and Margaret's pouty lips were not serviceable after hours. While my bourgeois wife settled into middle-class America, my longing for flesh and juice sent me out into the black haunts of the hood, where I met Diego.

I am not unsusceptible to guilt, despite the teaching of my church. I go to church every Sunday now – to a different church from Margaret's where thousands at a time worship the God of Victory in Technicolor triumph. My own church is of human scope and human creed yet cosmic, open, advanced. I enjoy the space and the approach to communion: practical food for the practical, adventurous nourishment for the brave or the curious, all at one and the same table. I am usually somewhere in the middle, but one Sunday I got carried away. Maybe I had read too much into the elder's call for honesty with God and self and other. But it spoke to my soul. To my soul's guilt. I was nostalgic for Margaret, for that evening that I have so often recollected. Her left foot, then her right, going from cold and damp to hot and twitching in my hands, in my mouth. The moment when the journey up her hard thighs ended at the stiff moist brush of her crotch. The pleasurable shock of her hot wetness seeping through my probing fingers. Me inside Margaret, unaccountably helpless and weeping from almost every orifice in my body.

I wanted it back, that moment of love, now that we were once again childless. So, foolishly, I told her everything. That everything which Diego, once my saviour, had called *not much, man!* The willing, fleshy women in the nightspots in the hood. The easy grooving. Vertical, then horizontal. In a motel, at their place, against a wall. No strings attached. Free love. It was love, because it was free, and easy and accepted. But, then again, maybe it wasn't love because it wasn't lasting.

Afterwards, I needed hands, again; soon, on my body. Unpaid hands. But all I had at my disposal were the paid hands of professional masseurs. I chose women, always, but it was never the same. All I wanted now were hands, generous hands, on my body. The guilt factor was functioning. I wanted to be the perfect son of a perfect father. Not a disappointment like John is to Margaret when she must admit, which she can't for ten minutes, that the son of her womb is gay.

I stopped sleeping with the women I danced with. I still wanted them, though, when we humped in the strobe lights with our clothes on. I disqualified sex to resemble my ideal. Decided that an exchange of massages was much, much better. I imitated the words of masseurs, I suggested that the woman of the moment strip to her degree of comfort. Fatally, I went for more than a giving of my hands in healing when it was my turn. Went for the flesh and the juice, imitating my grandmother's gourmandise. It had to stop. I confessed to Margaret; confessed fully. Cold hell broke loose. I thought I would die, till Diego saved me.

And now we are sitting in silence, each man in his own world because of twin whores, alias Alisha and Shawna, and the ideal of too much togetherness.

<hr>

Of course, you want to know what happened at Coco Beach. I am not sure myself. Maybe our stay at Coco Beach was like one of those long dreams, the kind that go on forever and stop and start again but last only a few minutes of clock time. Ten minutes after take-off, I had advanced little in my post-mortem. I had gone far, too far upstream. But since I've decided to go into this, I can't very well stop at 'I don't know, myself'. So, I'll tell it this way.

Diego had organized the whole thing; chosen the place, chosen the twins for the two of us – two men closer than brothers. The suites – communicating deluxe rooms – were really gorgeous. We had left our luggage in the gold room, as I had called it mentally because of the decor, with the communicating door open. Evening found us stretched out in companionable silence on either edge of the king-sized bed in the red room, nursing martinis. The twins delivered themselves to our door that Friday night at eight o'clock sharp. I had been basking in the luxury of the place and was now ready for a good dinner, a warm bath and bed. Basta! But the wine was drawn. The golden wine of identical twins who had grown different and had become easily distinguishable. Alisha: butter-yellow skin, direct gaze, royal blue skirt suit, generous décolleté, spicy perfume, high-heeled, open-toed pumps. Shawna: identical skin, pulpier, impression of an overripe fruit in a thick skin, white summer dress under a bolero, sandals, compensated by very formal make-up, lovely eyes, but a bit vacant, perfume imperceptible from the doorway. Maybe it was my over-long inspection of Shawna that had made her my choice? Or Alisha's frank once-over of Diego that appropriated him? The agenda of the evening was drinks and dinner at the first reasonable restaurant on the beach, then wild group party at our place. But from the word go the agenda shifted subtly beyond our control.

The outing went slowly. Diego had style. He was unrepentantly sensual, even gross, but he knew how to treat the ladies, bitches included. Of course, the term ladies and the distinction between them and bitches are mine. Diego doesn't do lofty, he just is. You would have thought that we were out on a date, two brothers dating two sisters and both sisters wanting the same brother to kiss them goodnight. Diego dined and wined and attended to the bitches in almost the same way that a gentleman treats the ladies, but with a tad more frankness in the gaze and touch, nothing extravagant. The food was good. The rum punches loosened me up. Shawna's professional hand was light on my thigh. It was time to go.

Diego and Alisha walked behind us on the beach, talking softly. Lingering. The night, too, was soft. The sisters held their shoes in their hands. Shawna breathed warmly, close by my side, encouraging. We breathed in unison. Apart, together, equally troubled. We could feel Diego and Alisha behind us. Our backs burned. We dared not turn around. We were dying to, our chests tight. There was silence now, except for the sigh of the breeze, I guess, and the suck of the waves. The bitch had bewitched my brother. It was a trite thought. A lump grew in my throat. It refused to move when I swallowed, a plug of sorrow grapes. But worse was to come.

Shawna was in the bathroom of the gold room, while the red room pulsated, dark and silent. An alcove. A planet.

In the gold room, far away, I was rooting my ass into the soft bed cover, flexing my neck and trying to get comfortable. I was coaching my breath, in the room that held our bags, Diego's and mine, heaped together, when the communicating door clicked shut, loud as a revolution.

I had lost my saviour.

Ineffectually, I mulled this over. I was numb, coaxing my breath into a hesitant calm. While Shawna spent forever in the bathroom, unmoored, excised, I rocked myself.

On the trip back home, high above the clouds, up-anchored from Diego, I search for my feet. From a bright carton, the flight attendant pours me mango juice in a beaker of brittle plastic. I decline the offer of ice. The orange-coloured juice gurgles forth, warm and bright. It is thick and sweet on my tongue. Earth and salt; sugar and spice, I think.

It tastes like the real thing.

Acknowledgements

Mahaman, you have no idea how much your support and admiration mean to me. I can't say it enough. Thank you! Maryam and Sarah, thanks for being my premier readers and vanguard supporters. Yes, the "club des malfaiteuses" is still going strong, although the fourth member, Karima, has left us, physically, for other climes.

Sulaiman, thank you for bringing these stories into the light. Throughout the process, you were thorough, professional, and thoughtful. Always demanding, ever kind. Where did you learn to be cautious and courageous at the same time?

To the sponsors, organisers and participants of 2014 Femrite Regional Residency for African Women Writers, a hearty thank you for the many benefits of my first residency experience at the Baltic Centre for Writers and Translators (Visby, Sweden). Thanks to the editors for choosing "Tina shot me between the eyes" for the residency anthology, *The Pot and Other Stories* and for readily agreeing to its inclusion in the present collection. Special thanks to Hilda Twongyeirwe for her blessings on this collection, to Ellen Banda Aaku for her mentorship during and after the residency and to Erik Falk for his kind support. I would like to acknowledge the entire team of Karavan who co-organised the residency. Thank you so much Birgitta Wallin for your priceless reassurance. To Lena Pasternak, gracious host at the Baltic Centre, I say: *tack så mycket*!

To Peter Espeut, Andrea Francis, Velma Pollard, Tana Silva and Hein Willemse: my heartfelt appreciation for the time you dedicated to reading some of these stories and for your invaluable comments.

Maria had the great idea of a prepublication reading of some of the stories at Sun Center in Gainesville, Florida summer 2016. Thank you, Leo and Monica Villalón, Susan Cooksey and other friends who attended this reading, for your affection and support.

Lightning Source UK Ltd.
Milton Keynes UK
UKOW04f0237170118
316288UK00001B/33/P